||||| ||| | || ||| ||| ||| |||
D0672409

Roofwalker

Roofwalker

SUSAN POWER

MILKWEED
EDITIONS

The characters and events in part one of this book are fictitious. Any similarity to real persons, living or dead, is coincidental and not intended by the author.

The author gratefully acknowledges the support of the editors who first published these stories in their journals and anthologies.

© 2002, Text by Susan Power
All rights reserved. Except for brief quotations in critical articles or reviews, no part of this book may be reproduced in any manner without prior written permission from the publisher: Milkweed Editions, 1011 Washington Avenue South, Suite 300, Minneapolis, Minnesota 55415.
(800) 520-6455
www.milkweed.org / www.worldashome.org

Published 2002 by Milkweed Editions
Printed in Canada
Cover and interior design by Dale Cooney
Cover painting, "Migrations," oil, 1996, by Ojibwe artist Jim Denomie
Author photo by Rebecca Dallinger
The text of this book is set in Legacy Serif.
02 03 04 05 06   5 4 3 2 1
First Edition

Special underwriting for *Roofwalker* was provided by an anonymous donor.

Milkweed Editions, a nonprofit publisher, gratefully acknowledges support from the Bush Foundation; General Mills Foundation; Marshall Field's Project Imagine with support from the Target Foundation; McKnight Foundation; Minnesota State Arts Board through an appropriation by the Minnesota State Legislature and a grant from the National Endowment for the Arts, and a grant from the Wells Fargo Foundation Minnesota; A Resource for Change technology grant from the National Endowment for the Arts; St. Paul Companies, Inc.; Target Stores; and generous individuals.

Library of Congress Cataloging-in-Publication Data

Power, Susan, 1961–
   Roofwalker / Susan Power.
      p. cm.
   ISBN 1-57131-039-8 (hardcover : alk. paper)
   1. Chicago (Ill.)—Fiction.   2. Indians of North America—Fiction.   I. Title.
   PS3566.O83578 R66 2002
   813'.54—dc21   2002006096

This book is printed on acid-free paper.

This one is for my sisters—

LeAnne Howe, Dawn Good Elk, and Elva Trevino Hart

Roofwalker

Stories

Histories

Roofwalker

Stories

Roofwalker

It was family legend that Grandma Mabel Rattles Chasing came down from the Standing Rock Reservation in North Dakota to help deliver me. She took the Greyhound bus all the way to Chicago, stepping out of the exhaust fumes like a ghost emerging from fog, her deep paper shopping bags banging against the sides of her legs. For most of the trip she had been finishing a child-sized star quilt, touching the fabric as gently as she would her new grandchild, smoothing it in her lap. This was the quilt they would wrap me in after my first bath, the same quilt Mom pulled out in later years every time I was sick.

Grandma Mabel came to help with the delivery because my mother was terrified of going to the huge maternity ward at Chicago's Cook County Hospital. She was convinced that the white doctors would sterilize her after she gave birth, a practice once routine at many reservation hospitals. So I was born in our third-floor apartment, which was little more than a chain of narrow rooms resembling the cars of a train.

Family legend continued that I began life with a fall. My birth went smoothly until Grandma Mabel wiped my face and head with her hands. What she saw made her scream, and I slipped out of her fingers like buttered dough. My father caught me. He went down on one knee, and his slim hands with long fingers stretched beneath me like a net.

"What is it?! What's wrong?!" I can imagine Mom's voice getting frantic as she tried to sit up, afraid I was born with too many fingers, or too few toes.

"Nothing, just her hair. It's different," Dad told her.

"The color of the devil," Grandma whispered, and they made her sit down because she was trembling.

As far back as anyone in my family could remember, both sides were Indian—full-blood Sioux on my mother's side and full-blood Sioux on my dad's. Yet I was born with red hair the color of autumn maple leaves. Grandma Mabel looked at me sideways and began to recite stories of the Viking invaders.

"Hundreds of years ago, long before Columbus and his three boats got lost and stumbled upon our land, those Vikings came down from the North country, where it's always cold. They had red hair and blue eyes, and heavy hatchets made of bronze. They married into our tribes. They must have. Just look." Grandma Mabel brushed my head with the tips of her fingers.

Although I was the mysterious family skeleton

pushed out of the closet with my mother's fluid still damp on my skin, Grandma Mabel didn't hold it against me for long. Soon she was cradling me in her broad lap, her round thighs ample as pillows. She traced my features with a thick finger, smoothing my forehead when it wrinkled in frustrated hunger. I know this because I have seen the photographs. I spent years playing with them, spreading them out on the coffee table. Grandma Mabel's skin was brown and wrinkled as a walnut, but her hair was mostly black, tied in one long braid. She wore shapeless cotton dresses and bowling sneakers, and I noticed that her legs looked strong but lumpy, a little like caked oatmeal. I knew her eyes were black because Mom told me, but in the photographs it was impossible to tell. Grandma Mabel's eyes were so bright they were beams of light shooting from her face, making me blink if I stared at them for too long.

Grandma Mabel was a presence in my life even though she returned to the reservation shortly after I was born. I came to know her through the photographs and the occasional phone calls she made from her tiny government-funded house. The stories she told me over the phone were better than the ones Mom told me at night before I fell asleep. Grandma asked me strange questions sometimes.

"Do you have spiders in Chicago?" she asked me once.

"Sure we do."

"I hope you don't kill them. You have to be careful because one of them might be Iktome."

"Who's that?" I asked her, smiling to myself because I knew the answer would involve a story.

"He is a spirit and sometimes he takes the form of a spider. He is clever-foolish, like your little brothers."

I knew what she meant. By this time I had two younger brothers, Billy and Grover, both of them as dark as our parents and Grandma Mabel, unburdened by my mysterious red hair, and both of them were energetically mischievous.

"Iktome is greedy," Grandma Mabel continued. "That's the bad side of him. If he has a plump duck or a haunch of venison set for dinner and he sees a chance to get something more, he will go after it. But you know what happens when he does that? Coyote sneaks behind him and steals the fat duck or the juicy venison and runs off with it. Then Iktome goes hungry."

"Grandma, I wish you were here," I told her one time. I wanted the stories to last longer. I wanted her shining eyes to light my room at bedtime like two candles burning in the dark.

"I know it," she said. "It's hard."

❧ ❧

"Why do we live in Chicago?" I finally asked my mother after one particularly entertaining visit with Grandma

Mabel, when she told me she could hear her husband's ghost singing to her from the bottom of their old well.

"Your father's job is here," Mom told me.

"Can't he work somewhere else?"

"It's not that easy." Mom sighed. "He's a political person, and political people don't always have a lot of choices."

My mother chose her words cautiously, I could tell. She spoke slowly, and the words seemed heavy as she spoke them, like dense marbles rolling off her tongue. There were other times when she flung words at my father and wasn't careful at all. She'd point to him and tell us: "Your father is a gung ho Indian. It's his job and his life!"

We were living in the uptown area of Chicago, just blocks away from the Indian Center on Wilson Avenue, which is where Dad went to work each day. I knew that he wrote proposals for the Indian community, but when I was little I didn't understand what that meant. I imagined my father writing marriage proposals for shy Indian men who couldn't find the words for themselves, who would have spent their lives alone were it not for my father's intervention. Likewise, I didn't know what a gung ho Indian was, but in retrospect, I suppose my father fits that description. He always wore jeans, cowboy boots, a western shirt with silver clips on the collar, and a heavy turquoise bolo tie. He never carried a briefcase but instead used an old backpack completely covered by pins and bumper stickers with slogans like CUSTER DIED FOR YOUR SINS, I'M SIOUX AND PROUD, INDIAN POWER, and POWWOW COUNTRY.

Dad burned tobacco on Columbus Day to mourn the arrival of the man who pressed Indians into slavery, fasted on Thanksgiving Day to show his solidarity with all those eastern tribes the Pilgrims killed off with their European strain of germs, and set off fireworks on June 26 to celebrate the anniversary of the Little Big Horn battle, when our ancestors crushed Custer like a wood tick.

I asked Grandma Mabel what it all meant.

"What is a gung ho Indian?"

"Well . . ." She paused then, and I could hear her sipping liquid, probably wild peppermint tea, which she said kept her blood healthy. "That's a good question. It used to be that your people knew who they were and what was expected of them. From the time they were born, each day was a lesson. They were close to the father over all of us, *Wakan Tanka,* the one who hears our prayers. But we have gone through many things, and now it's difficult to find the right road. Some of our people try too hard; they think they've found the old-time trail leading them to the heart of our traditions, but if they looked down, I think they would see only their footprints. It is their own lonely trail, and they are truly lost."

Was my father lost? I wanted to call him back and take him by the hand. I would walk with him, eyes cast upon the ground, looking for signs that other Sioux people had passed this way before us. I didn't want him to wander all alone, carrying nothing but his worn backpack and an angry heart.

~ ~

When I was nine years old, Dad left us. My brothers and I were like those three blind mice: we didn't see it coming. I think my mother did. I am certain now that Mom could read this future in my father's face, because when the time came, she simply lived through it. She had probably noticed the way women watched my handsome father, who was tall and straight with brown skin smooth as glass and wavy long hair streaming down his back.

Of course, Dad didn't tell us there was another woman but blamed politics for our separation. He said he was going back to his own reservation in South Dakota, Pine Ridge, where so much trouble was brewing.

"I can make a difference," he said.

My mother wasn't fooled for a second. "Then take us with you," she told him.

"It's not that easy," my father answered. "These days Pine Ridge is dangerous, Indians fighting Indians and the FBI just complicating everything. I can't take you back there."

Dad bought a used Volkswagen van and painted bronze fists on each of its sides. At first I admired it, imagined it reflected his conscience and principles; it was a rugged little vehicle, hell-bent for danger and activism. But then my mother pointed out the truth with her chin as we watched it from our apartment window. My father had a young girl with hair as long as his own already living in that van.

I decided to investigate, and when Mom was busy preparing lunch for me and my brothers, I ran down the front stairs. The girl was standing outside the van, leaning against it with her arms crossed. She was watching our apartment windows three stories above her with muddy green eyes the color of the Chicago River. She's only a part-blood Indian, like me, I thought. She had on hip-hugger jeans with wide bell-bottoms that dragged on the ground, covering her feet. On top she wore a skimpy halter hanging loosely from her narrow, caved-in chest. I knew she was observing me, too, although she never glanced away from the window. I was in the doorway of our building, right in front of her, staring rudely, which I had been taught never to do.

Finally she asked, "Which one are you?"

"Jessie," I told her. I pulled myself a little straighter and wiped the limp red bangs from my forehead.

"Oh," she said. She shrugged her right shoulder and lifted suddenly on tiptoes to get a better view of our apartment. Just as I was about to leave, pushing back against the outside glass door, she looked at me again. Her green eyes fell on mine like heavy hammers. I couldn't blink, my eyes were dry, her hard look was squeezing the breath from my lungs. My fingernails cut into my palms.

"I love him," she said. We stood there silently for a while.

Finally I whispered, "I love him too." My voice was gentle, but it wasn't out of kindness or sympathy. Anger sizzled in the pit of my stomach; I felt the sparks fly inside of me, scorching my heart and lungs. She turned her back on me, retreating into the safety of the van.

I walked to the back of the building and sat on the porch steps. I wished I could become a bird of vengeance. I curled my toes inside my sneakers, feeling their terrible grip, and imagined the fierce sweep they would make at that part-blood girl's hair. My talons would tangle in her hair like barbed wire and I would carry her off, banging her useless, scrawny body against the buildings as I flew toward the lake. Halfway to Canada maybe I would let her go, hovering in the air so I could watch her fall into the deep cold center of Lake Michigan. Her heavy, angry eyes would weight her down like stones. She would never float or be recovered.

As the bird of vengeance, I would shriek and cackle loud enough that my mother would hear it and know she was avenged, powerful enough that my father would hear me and know that I had won.

The day finally came for my father to leave. My mother sat on one of the kitchen chairs. For the first time I noticed that the chair she always used was the one repaired with black electrical tape, just as she always set herself the chipped plate and bent fork. Dad was standing with one pointy-toed boot resting on a chair, his body hitched over the bent knee. My parents faced slightly apart, and I remember worrying that they wouldn't be able to hear each other, that their words would slide in different directions.

"Let's not put the kids through a big scene," Dad told her.

Mom's dry eyes hurt me more than if they had been pouring tears like the Hoover Dam burst open. She didn't flinch or rustle but was suddenly still and massive, the center of gravity become flesh in our kitchen.

"It doesn't matter what I say or what I do," she finally said, and I was convinced that her voice slipped out of her navel and not from her thin, pressed lips.

Was that all she was going to say? I was trembling, as nervous as she was motionless; my blood was sliding too quickly through my veins. I wanted to scream, *Stop him! Don't let him go!* But I had been raised too well for that. Instead I bit my tongue until I tasted blood.

Dad moved then, walked toward my mother. He scooped her hand into his but almost lost it, it was so heavy.

"You're a good woman," he said, "and I promise I'll call you. Take care of yourself." He kissed her on the cheek and replaced her hand. He was on his way out. He looked so relieved when he said his last words: "I just have to do some things that are bigger than my life."

"Don't kid yourself," Mom answered.

I know Dad must have hugged and kissed the three of us before he made it out the front door. After all, we stood there in the hallway between the kitchen and living room, his last hurdle to freedom. But I don't remember it. I must have blanked the moment out. Or maybe I was frightened because his last touch was too much like a ghost walking right through me.

I remember looking out of the front window, my mother suddenly beside me. She took my hand and I realized she was facing the wrong way, her back to the street.

"Has he gone?" she asked me. I looked out and saw the painted upraised fists slide away from our building. The rear fender gleamed when Dad stopped for a red light at the corner, and as he turned there was a flash, like the winking of an eye.

"Yes," I told her, "I can't see him anymore."

"Then that's the last time," she said, moving heavily toward the kitchen.

Roofwalker · 15

Dad left on July 1. The very next day a heat wave hit Chicago, which seemed associated with the hole in the world Dad left behind. There was an imbalance to things; we had lost our equilibrium and were living at extremes. With a large ice cube in my mouth, I practiced freezing my heart. Mom didn't bother to sit near a fan or wipe the sweat from her forehead with the towel I draped around her neck.

"Are you hungry?" I asked her because I was, and my brothers were chewing on dry cereal while they watched the *Three Stooges.* She didn't answer or even act as if she heard me. A tear of sweat rolled from her temple to the curve of her jawline and on down her neck to soak into her red tank top.

"Do you think he'll come back?" I asked her. The fingers of her right hand twitched, but that was her only response.

"C'mon." I herded my brothers into the kitchen and cut them slices of Colby cheese. We ate cheese and buttery Ritz crackers for lunch and later for dinner.

That week my mother became her own ghost, and I became more real. I learned to heat SpaghettiOs in a pan on the dark metal burners and to light the oven to heat up chicken potpies. At night I wiped my brothers' foreheads with ice wrapped in a washcloth and made sure the fan was blowing straight onto their small forms. It was a week of heat, quiet, and solitude.

Mom came back to us a little at a time. One night

she laughed at something on TV, and we all came running to laugh with her. "What is it, Mom? What's so funny?" I sat on the edge of her easy chair and put my arm around her damp shoulder.

"Hmmm?" She peered at the three of us, taking stock, and we moved instinctively closer like wealth to be counted. Billy planted his hands on her knees and rocked toward her face.

"We heard you," he whispered, and then he laughed out loud because she bumped her nose against his. "Eskimo kiss!" Billy shouted.

～ ～

One week had passed. My brothers found solace in Tonka trucks and a G.I. Joe with a furry crew cut and kung fu grip. I trailed after my mother, determined to ward off her unhappiness with my vigilance. One evening we sat together. It was later than it looked. We had all the windows pushed open as wide as they would go.

"An inch of breeze is an inch of breeze," Mom had said as we helped her tug on window sashes warped by the heat.

I sat across from Mom at the kitchen table. She was doing the *TV Guide* crossword puzzle, and I was pretending to color pictures in a coloring book while I was really keeping an eye on her.

"What's the name of that guy from *Little House on the*

Prairie?" she asked me, the tip of her pen waving over the paper.

"Michael Landon," I said. "He plays the pa."

That made her look up before she finished writing his name, and she glanced at my artwork. She moved her arms, about to get up from the table, but her skin was warm and stuck to the Formica. My arms were stuck, too, and when I finally pulled them free, they were greasy, coated with toast crumbs.

Mom laughed. "Now you know what a bug stuck to flypaper feels like." Then she cocked her head at the silence. "Say, what are your brothers up to? They've been too quiet." Mom left to find Billy and Grover after wiping her arms with a dish towel. The kitchen was darker all of a sudden. I could hear cicadas thrumming from the vacant lot next door, and I had this sad, loose-ends feeling of wasted time.

Mom came back into the kitchen, brandishing her red patent-leather purse. She waved it in the air, saying, "Let's make us some black cows!" So the four of us went to the corner liquor store, where we bought vanilla ice cream, root beer, and striped plastic straws for our floats. But Grover said he wanted his ice cream in Coke, so then Billy wanted Coke too. Mom made a face but she let them switch their A&Ws for Cokes.

On the way back Mom spotted a thick patch of milkweed as high as her waist in the vacant lot. "Look at this," she said. She reached out her free hand to gauge the weight of green pods heavy with latex. "Just what you kids need, some green in your diet." Mom handed me the black cow fixings, starting to break out of the moist bottom of the paper bag, and put the keys in my pocket.

"Why don't you run this up before it melts and then come back? I'm going to collect some of these greens." By the time I returned it was almost dark and her arms were full of thick-stemmed milkweeds looking like an exotic bridal bouquet.

Grover and Billy were picking around by the Dumpster so I went to collect them. "Look, Jessie," Grover hissed. He pulled Billy out of the way so I could see. Some winos were passed out in the space between the Dumpster and the brick wall of our building. The smell rising from their niche was worse than that coming from the open garbage. I couldn't count how many there were—maybe three or four—because they were piled in a confusion of dirty clothes, their legs stacked together like wood.

"Get away from there!" Mom called us back and hefted the plants higher in her arms. "Leave those poor drunks alone. Let them sleep it off in peace."

"Are they dead?" Billy asked me as we followed Mom and the cluster of milk flowers nodding over her shoulder.

"No," I said, "they're just sleeping." I could tell Billy didn't believe me. I heard him whisper to Grover when we were walking up the stairs: "Dad wouldn't of left those dead Indians to get eaten by flies."

We both hushed him.

～　～

Dad had been gone exactly two weeks and Mom was making sounds about the future. She said, "With me going back to work, you'll have more responsibilities."

Her fingers were smoothing out a white athletic sock, one of Dad's. She caught me watching her and quickly balled the sock into a tight wad, chucking it basketball style into the tall kitchen trash can. She pressed her empty hands against the table and smiled. "Everything's going to be okay, though. It'll be all right."

"I know," I told her.

My mother held her arms out to me in a way she hadn't done since I was as young as my brothers. I moved hesitantly, but she pulled me onto her lap, and our bare legs, poking out of polyester shorts, slid together like held hands.

"I guess you're not too young for me to talk to real serious."

I couldn't see her; we were both facing the refrigerator door, taped all over with poems cut out of Indian newspapers like *News from Indian Country* and *Akwesasne*

Notes. The printing was so small that from across the room it looked like trails of sugar ants crawling up and down. Mom talked over my shoulder, her warm breath sliding past my neck.

"Listen up now," she began, but interrupted herself. She leaned against me to bury her face in my hair. "Boy, it sure smells sweet," Mom said, "and it's real pretty. Always was pretty." I knew she meant my unusual red hair.

"See." She was holding pale strands near the window, where they glistened in the sunlight. "It's just like Black Hills gold. Three different colors woven together." Mom paused, my hair held close to her eyes. She was suddenly very quiet, and I could feel tears gathering in the air.

"I want to tell you something, okay? Just because your father took off on some crazy adventure doesn't mean he stopped caring about us. He's just mixed up. He thinks he's doing the right thing, but he's forgetting that a Sioux man's first duty is to his family." Mom was crying now, her tears falling on my thighs like the first warning drops of rain. "Do you hear me?"

I nodded and swallowed my own throat again and again. *Don't defend him,* I wanted to tell her, but I remained silent. I stroked Mom's hand with my fingers. I was tired of seeing my mother rub away, becoming so thin the few wrinkles on her forehead pulled taut across

the bone, her face as smooth as the worry stones I saw
between the fingers of old women in Greektown.

～ ～

Grandma Mabel came for a visit that summer, smelling
faintly of sweet grass. She entered our apartment gracefully. Her ancient carpetbag (which she said dated back
to the Truman administration), heavy support hose,
and worn bowling sneakers did not detract from her air
of dignity.

I meant to give Grandma a tour of our apartment
when I took her hand, leading her from room to room.
But along the way she took over and began labeling familiar objects. She pointed to my parents' bedside table,
its one short leg propped higher with a *Reader's Digest*.

She said, *"Waglutapi,"* and dropped her hand.
Grandma paused, looking at me.

"Waglutapi?" I repeated. Grandma nodded.
She pointed to the door: *"Tiyopa";* the window,
"Ozanzanglepi." In the kitchen she poked her finger
at the dingy stove. *"Oceti,"* she said. Billy had left a soda
can on the kitchen table and Grandma snatched it,
waving it before my face. *"Kapopapi,"* she told me, wig-
gling her eyebrows. It had a funny sound. I couldn't say
it correctly because each time I tried, I sputtered laugh-
ter. Pretty soon the two of us were holding each other
for support, Grandma shaking and shaking with light,

almost soundless gasps that wafted like smoke rings to the ceiling.

"Oh, I've got to pee," she finally managed, and rushed past me to the bathroom. I'd never seen an old lady move so quickly.

At night the two of us shared my bed, across the room from where my little brothers slept in a tangle of bony elbows. Grandma wore white cotton anklets to bed.

"When you get old the blood doesn't reach your feet anymore," she explained. And she never wore a real nightgown. Instead she pulled on one of her old house-dresses, worn away almost to gauze, the print on the fabric washed off long ago. She had a set of rosary beads that glowed in the dark. She wore them around her neck and they glared at me like little eyes unless I slept with my back to her.

After saying her prayers in Sioux, she would pull me against her, a heavy arm draped across my waist. The smell of sweet grass was so thick in the bed I imagined we were sleeping on the plains.

It was Grandma Mabel who told me about the roof-walker. "My *tunkasila,* that's my grandfather, first saw the roofwalker standing in the sky, his wings stretched so wide he covered the light of the moon and most of the stars. My *tunkasila* said the roofwalker was born out of misery, right after the Wounded Knee massacre, where so many of our people were killed for holding a

Ghost Dance. They were buried in the snow and the roofwalker drifted over their mass grave, his eyes big and hungry, so empty my *tunkasila* hunched in the snow, afraid he would be eaten.

"And now that roofwalker has followed me to Chicago. Isn't he crazy? He'll get lost and never find the Dakotas again. He'll choke over those steel mills or fly straight into that John Hancock Building, won't he?"

Grandma tickled me with her stubby fingers and we almost rolled out of the bed with our giggling. To finish her story, however, Grandma became serious. She whispered as if the roofwalker were listening. I kept glancing at the window, expecting to see the smoky steam of his breath, but the window was clear black.

She told me that the roofwalker was a Sioux spirit, a kind of angel. "He isn't good or bad, though," she said. "He just is."

The roofwalker was the hungriest of all spirits, hugely, endlessly hungry, his stomach an empty cavern of echoes.

"You see," Grandma explained, "even though he's starving, he is fussy. Always holding out for a delicacy."

The roofwalker lived to eat dreams, and when he feasted on the dream of his choice, it always came true. "Did he ever get one of yours?" I asked Grandma Mabel, trying to imagine what a dream tasted like, and how you could fit it in your mouth without choking.

"Yes, he did," she said. She smoothed the hair off my forehead. "I dreamed you."

I let my head fall back against Grandma's chest. I could feel her rosary beads tangle in my hair and rub against my scalp. I dreamt that we were sleeping on the prairie, Grandma's fingers pointing out the stars, her arms so long she could reach up and dust them.

～ ～

That fall, after Grandma Mabel returned to North Dakota, her voice remained in my head, repeating stories and Sioux vocabulary words. I think that is why the creature came to me. He stepped full grown from my dreams, a night visitor prowling through my thoughts, and later, quite fleshed out, hovering outside my bedroom window as if treading air. My brothers slept on in the next bed that night. I could see their gray outline and the hang of loose arms, thin as sticks.

I wanted to wake them, to ask them, "Do you see him out there? Has he gone?" But I didn't. Instead I admired the creature's brown, hairless body, glistening and smooth. He seemed eager, his mouth open and barbed tongue curled over his teeth. His eyes were penetrating, the black pupils drilled; I was convinced he could see right through my brain and spot my dreams. I knew what that tongue was for. I knew what he did. The tiny curved thorns lining the edge of his tongue like needles were for catching dreams. His tongue was flexible enough for excavation, like delicate surgery, and after he swallowed an extracted dream, it would come true.

I wasn't surprised that he looked just like my father, although his thick waist-length hair was trimmed with feathers. The handsome face and the strong arms and torso were my father's. Only the legs were different: feathered haunches, and curved talons for feet.

"You are part bird," I whispered to him through the pane of glass separating us. "You are part spirit." His eyes stared without expression, but his hand lifted a necklace worn against his chest, which was strung with bear claws, elk teeth, and rare dentalium shells. I tried to reach my hand through the glass to stroke the necklace he proffered with a graceful hand, but as I grazed the barrier, he flew upward, and I heard a backwash of wind forced by the beating of powerful wings.

In the morning I looked for scattered red and black feathers, the color of his plumage. I couldn't find any, but that didn't shake my faith. I knew the roofwalker had visited me. He was as real as I needed him to be.

~ ~

When I was little I had blind faith in family legends, my grandmother's stories, and even in my handsome father, who was temporarily lost, searching for the road Grandma Mabel told me was beneath my own feet.

After all, he had been the one to catch me before I slipped to the floor, the one who kept me in the world once my mother released me.

Grandma Mabel told me that life is a circle, and sometimes we coil around on ourselves like a drowsy snake. Weeks after Grandma Mabel returned to North Dakota, I decided to circle back to my own beginning. Perhaps that was where I should go to make things right, to bring my father home to his lonesome family. It seemed very clear to me what I had to do.

It was my tenth birthday. I woke before anyone else and dressed quietly so I wouldn't wake my brothers. I looked out of the front window and watched the leaves fall, tugged loose by a morning wind. I slipped out of the front door but left it unlocked for my return.

I chose the place carefully, somewhere high enough to test faith, but not so high as to be dangerous. I stood at the top of the final flight of stairs leading to our tiled vestibule. I was ten carpeted steps away from the front door of our building. I curled the edges of my feet over the top step, feeling the space slope forward and downward. I lunged chin first into the fall with eyes closed, my body as relaxed as the startled release of tension before sleep. I waited for Dad to catch me, for the roofwalker to throw back his head and open his mouth, letting my dream float up from his throat into the breeze rolling away from Lake Michigan.

Watermelon Seeds

Sometimes I want to take this baby out of me before it's alive and breathing and wanting too much. Catch it before it grows from being a seed. I never wanted Donald to put this baby in me. It's hard enough just the two of us.

"This goddamn kid is doomed," Donald says around a long swig of beer he takes in like air and breathes out like a malt dragon. "This kid is going to be so screwed up I can hear it already. Damn, can't you shut it up?!"

If I ever snatched that brown glass bottle from Donald's mouth, stripped his lips and told him—*I don't want it either! I don't want it fighting me in there!*—I know *what* would hit the fan. I'd break the sound barrier, flying off the end of Donald's broken fist.

I curl up sometimes with one hand on my stomach, whispering things like, "I'll make you grilled cheese sandwiches," because I have these dreams where I can hear the baby crying. It is curled around my intestines and holding on with hands smaller than a silver dollar.

The baby shakes its wizened Donald face and tells me it won't come out. No way.

~ ~

"Bagged at sixteen, that's really sad," my mother told me just last week, with chicken-greasy fingers poked in her mouth. She should know, she had me when she was that age. She would never say that kind of thing in front of Donald, but we were in her kitchen, sharing cold left-over chicken and sorting through coupons with five city blocks between Mama's mouth and Donald's ears.

She used to come over to our place nearly every morning for breakfast, reading us our "Omarr's Horo-scope" from the *Chicago Sun-Times,* but now I go over to her apartment after setting out Donald's bacon strips and burned grits because Donald says it starts his day off wrong to see me sitting across the kitchen table like an expectant cow. As if he goes off to work and has a rough day. He doesn't. We live off his disability and the beadwork he taught me to do, which we sell at pow-wows from Michigan to Minnesota. Donald advertises the beadwork as his own because he's a Chippewa Indian from Lac du Flambeau, Wisconsin, while I'm Mexican from Dad's side and Polish from Mama's.

"Nobody wants to buy any Taco-Polack stuff," Donald says. "They want genuine Indian shit, so keep to my designs."

In a hatbox way in back of my side of the closet I keep a collection of secret work. I use tiny cut seed beads that sparkle to sew the pictures, stringing just three beads at a time like Donald taught me. I wear a thimble on each finger to help shove the needle through the leather; it can tear up your fingers to do this kind of work.

I hide my beaded pictures because they aren't Indian designs like Donald wants, but a reflection of what I see in our neighborhood, what some people call the Chicago Hills—the white trash ghetto Ozarks in the uptown area. There are Indians and Puerto Ricans, but mostly hillbillies living around here, just a few evil-smelling blocks from Lake Michigan and all the big white boats docked at Belmont Harbor. One of my beaded pictures is a scene of Donald burning one of those boats, a really big one. He hasn't ever burned a boat but he talks about how good it would feel to sink one out of sight. He says, "Strike one for the good guys," and tips his beer bottle toward the east where all those boats are tied down and covered up. I don't know what he means. I don't even know why he's one of the good guys.

When I try to draw him out, try to understand him better the way those psychologists on *Oprah Winfrey* say you should before you give up on a person, I stub my toes. Donald won't talk much about his growing-up years.

"You want to hear a litany of self-pity, go over to your mother's," he told me when I asked about his past. Sometimes when he's way into the bottle, on a real bender, he mumbles a detail or two. So I know he and his brothers did a lot of spearfishing to keep food on the table and might have even speared game of the two-legged variety—a stepfather whose name he cries out in his sleep. Carter. I'm still trying to piece that story together.

I asked him once why he left Wisconsin for Chicago and he told me, "You can get lost in the city, so they hate you less."

I wrote it down in my red diary locked with a gold key, but no matter which way I look at it, I don't understand. At least Donald gave me a picture of himself taken when he was my age. He is so handsome in that picture, with thick black hair greased and combed high off his forehead, the short sleeves of his T-shirt rolled back to show off his muscles. He is a full-blood Indian version of Elvis in that picture, and the Donald I will always love. My eyes have learned to carve him out of the man I live with.

Donald is thirty years old but looks older because his wrinkles are deep as cracks in a pounded wall. I know from his nightmares that his stepfather is responsible for a lot of the hammering he has taken. His hard drinker's belly rides over the beaded belt buckle I made him for Valentine's Day. His stomach squirms and rumbles like his insides are angry.

Donald is impulsive, something Mama is still trying to account for because it contradicts the description of his Taurus sign as taciturn, measured, slow to action. I think Mama's been looking for a freakish alignment of planets at the time of his birth. He switches back and forth on me, like the night I told him about the baby. At first he bellowed. He kept saying, "It will *never* work, it will *never* work." But then the next morning I woke up in the bed alone, my feet covered with what felt like a mound of cookie crumbs. I pulled down the covers on Donald's side of the bed and stared. Donald had uprooted clusters of plum-colored hydrangea bushes and placed them beside me. The flowers were full and fat as pom-poms, springing from perfect green leaves shaped like spades in a deck of cards. The roots, still clinging soil, tangled at the bottom like wild blond hair.

I heard Donald in the kitchen humming "Spanish Eyes" while he made me breakfast. I guess he had forgiven me and the baby. At least for a time.

~ ~

Technically, we're not starving. Donald gets a disability check from the Army for when a new recruit shot him in the thigh at target practice and messed up the big bone in there. That and the little bit I make from beadwork keep us in flour and vegetable oil for fry bread, and dark beans and lean hamburger for my endless chili. But today I want a triangle of pork chop as thick as my thumb to surprise Donald. I know he'll smell it from the landing four flights down. It will urge him upstairs, getting stronger and stronger, hitting him like a meat cloud outside our door.

The grease will still be lining his mouth and oiling the tips of his fingers when he comes to bed, smelling the smoke in my hair. We will kiss the flavor off each other until Donald falls asleep with his forehead laid flat against my neck, an easy expression unwrinkling him. At least, that's how it should be.

When I imagine the pork chops and me in an apron with my hair twisted up, eyes turned soft brown under daubs of pearl pink eyeshadow, I find myself staking out Water Tower Place on the Magnificent Mile. I have on my ugliest jeans and fastest sneakers. I am watching the ghosts shop.

A pair of women who must be mother and daughter are looking in the I. Magnin shop window, a block away from Water Tower Place. The mother is saying, "Don't get too many miniskirts. Next season you just *know* they'll lower the hemlines and you'll have to go out and start from scratch. That's no way to build an efficient wardrobe."

The daughter rolls her eyes. It looks like she doesn't have on any makeup so I know she wears the expensive kind of cosmetics, the perfumed kind as subtle as disappearing ink.

All up and down this section of Michigan Avenue that looks like it spills right into the lake at its end, I see people straight out of nighttime soaps like *Dynasty* or *Falcon Crest*. They are too perfect for me to take seriously. Their hair and nails are so neat, so polished, they are like aliens who have taken the place of the real thing. Michigan Avenue is *Invasion of the Body Snatchers* all over. It's spooky.

I'm ready for action. I am near invisible but all-powerful. I can feel my heart beating in my throat, my chest, at my wrists, even whamming down by my ankles. I have the fastest feet in the world. I wait patiently and carefully; it's important to find the right purse belonging to the right lady. Just when I think I'll never find her, she walks straight in front of me. She is perfect— young, beautiful, tall. She smells wonderful and attracts the stares of men, who turn their heads to watch her pass.

For a few heart-slamming moments I take control of her life. I step on her shadow and touch her shoulder. She thinks I'm some guy making a pass. I let her take one good startled look at my face before I grasp the leather handle of her purse and pull for my life. The bag is suede, as soft as the beautiful lady's moisturized skin. I am half a block away before she gets her voice back, and there is no catching me now.

I take the purse to a pretty little gazebo in Lincoln Park and sit with my legs crossed, pretending the purse is mine. I casually go through its contents and discover a whole life in that purse. An hour earlier I didn't know its owner and she didn't know me, but now I'm reading her as plainly as a gypsy reads palms.

I like the photographs best. There's a stack of them in the wallet, pictures of her parents and boyfriend. She even has old school pictures of herself going back to when she had braces and oily skin. I think of my own school pictures Mama arranged on her wall, going around in a circle like a clock. The picture from tenth grade ends up next to the one from kindergarten like I'll jump from being fifteen to age five. That's probably the way Mama thinks I'm living my life.

I keep the money but decide to mail the purse and its contents back to the owner, to the address on her driver's license. I don't even keep the credit cards or the little gold locket on a broken chain I find in a zippered pocket. It adds a whole new dimension to my power to return what I have taken. This is the way Donald must feel when he cries me an apology.

꩜

I'm three months pregnant when Mama surprises me. She really lets me have it. Usually she keeps her opinions to herself, partly out of habit from the days when my father was still alive, and partly because she says kids will always do the opposite of what you tell them.

I go over to her place really early for breakfast. She looks up from the astrology column when I walk in. Her look pins me in the doorway. I cross my arms in front of my chest but that doesn't help because my arms are striped with blue welts. They look like fancy twirling batons.

Mama grabs me and drags me into the bathroom. Her palm pushes against the back of my head, supporting it at the base, the way a mother cups the head of a baby so it doesn't wobble loosely on its neck.

"Look. Take a good look at yourself!" she yells. She pushes my head so close to the cabinet mirror my breath makes curls of steam. "How do you like it? Your eye all out to here? You're just so attractive, Lois. You take my breath away."

After she says that she leaves me, taking away her hand. My whole body goes limp like a rubber band shot against the wall, and I fall to the ground. For a long time the only important thing is staying on the cool tile floor, counting the six sides of each tile and studying how they fit together, feeling the grit against my cheek. I don't ever have to get up off the floor again.

Mama comes back after a while and sits on the edge of the tub. I'm looking at her open-toed slippers. Purple frost nail polish is chipping off her toenails. She sighs, and I close my eyes so I can stay curled up at her feet.

"I don't mean to make it worse," she says. "It pisses me off. I guess I feel responsible because it's what you saw with me and that S.O.B. father of yours. But I wouldn't take it off him now, okay? You hear me? No way I'd stand for that shit now."

Mama leaves, and I have the feeling she will never say anything about this again.

I want to tell her it's fate that brought Donald and me together, so I guess it's fate that will work out the ending, not her. She doesn't even know the whole story.

~ ~

I didn't go back to school after some hillbillies got me in the girl's bathroom and did a job on me. The heavy one, JoJo, with sharp overlapping teeth and a hacksaw haircut, sat on my back and held me down while Ginny and Melora used toenail clippers to cut my hair. After that they poured bleach on my head and turned my brown hair a brittle yellow white the color of grapefruit pulp.

"You ever seen a white Mexican before?" JoJo pulled me up by the collar and turned me around so I faced Ginny and Melora's teeth and gums, shoved out of their mouths like laughing fools. HAW HAW HAW. The bleach burned the skin on my neck and scalp, and I had to wipe my forehead to keep it from drizzling into my eyes.

"She looks so bad she could be arrested for being in

public," said Ginny, and when they doubled over with giggles, I took off. I never even went back to open up my locker and get some tapes I had in there, good dance tapes it took forever to make off WLS Radio.

Mama cut my hair better and evened the yellow until it grew out, but for a while there my skinny face looked just like the death mask she has hanging on her living room wall. It is a mask of my father's face, made after his heart attack and before his cremation. Mama says she needs all the proof she can get that he is dead, dead, dead, so she keeps his ashes in an old plastic Cool Whip bowl under her bed and his death mask on the wall over the TV set. One of her boyfriends punched a hole in the mask between the lips and stuck a cigarette in there. I don't like it, because it makes him look like he is alive, pushing right through the wall and coming after us.

Donald started out as one of my mother's boyfriends, but I took him over. He wasn't working, and I wasn't leaving for school like Mama thought. The minute she left for her waitressing job I set him up with a beer and we watched cartoons together. Pretty soon Donald was making time with me in my bed.

"It's more comfortable in there," he said once, nodding toward Mama's room, but it was bad enough I stole him away. I wouldn't use her bed. Donald was shy and wouldn't ever undress all the way, although he liked me stripped like a little stick.

Mama didn't forgive me and Donald for falling in love behind her back until we moved out and got our own place. Then she was full of advice and always coming over with fancy recipes she'd never tried herself, or material for matching bedspreads and curtains. She even took out a Sears charge card and helped us buy some furniture.

"I want you to do it right," she explained when I asked her why she was helping. "You're starting too early, just like me. But maybe with people behind you from the get-go, you'll make it."

Mama wasn't as understanding when I told her I was pregnant. I really hadn't meant to ruin her day, but I had to warn her about the baby, like it was a coming attraction she wouldn't want to miss. Maybe I picked a bad time. Mama was all excited about a blind date she was going on later that evening. A real date with dinner and a movie and dressing up. She asked me over to watch her model clothes and help her pick out a dress that might change her whole future.

She was taking her hair out of tight curls pinned to her head, scattering bobby pins and looking vulnerable with half her hair stuck like glue to her scalp and half of it hanging down in corkscrew ringlets. She looked for a second like she would understand, so I opened my mouth. I repeated something I'd read in a science textbook: "The species will propagate."

It stopped Mama dead in her tracks. "What are you talking about?" She suddenly noticed the bobby pins and stooped to collect them.

"I'm having a baby."

Mama took air down the wrong pipe and choked. I started forward to slap her on the back, but she pulled away. She threw the bobby pins right at me, in a shower, the way people chuck rice at a wedding. Mama and I fell into a black hole of time that felt like *The Twilight Zone*. We didn't move or speak. Finally Mama snapped her head to the side. She was looking at my school pictures circling on her wall.

"Well, I either accept it or I don't," she said, mostly to herself. "There's no going back now." She flicked the bangs out of my eyes so she could stare at me.

"Aren't you the typical Pisces?" she sighed. "Flaky, dreamy, never living in the real world. But here's the kicker, Lois, baby. Now the real world's got itself *right in you.*"

~ ~

In July Donald decides to go back to Lac du Flambeau for a visit. I want him to take me with him and introduce me to his family, but he won't.

"Nah," he says, "my ma would just get on me for robbing the cradle."

"Will you tell them about the baby?"

Donald is packing his old Army duffle bag. He rolls his clothes very tightly so it looks like his bag is full of snakes and sausages. He shakes his head, no.

"We're not married. What am I going to say? *Hey, I'm shacked up with this goofy Mexican and about to have a kid?* Don't be squirrelly."

That's when I get my idea. If Donald hadn't accused me of being squirrelly it wouldn't have occurred to me. The day he leaves it rains, so I can't carry out my plan, but the day after that is perfect. The sun is high and bright, the clouds have all been swept to Canada. Gray-backed seagulls from the lake glide over buildings like wisps of smoke.

I wear one of Mama's old bikinis under a T-shirt and shorts, and pack myself a towel. At Murray's Market I buy a *Teen Magazine*. I roll it in the towel because its pages are slick and shiny, and I don't want to smudge them with my sweaty hands. I'm almost four months pregnant but still not showing. That much is obvious when I get to Oak Street Beach and peel off the shirt and shorts. I am sharing the sand with hundreds of people my age who don't even suspect that I'm an intruder. I'm not what I seem. Flopped on my stomach to read *Teen Magazine* without the sun glaring in my eyes, I forget the second heartbeat pulsing in my belly.

A bunch of kids who go to Francis Parker Academy— an elite school—invite me to play volleyball with them.

Volleyball was my game before I left high school. I enjoy the way the ball smacks against the inside of my arms, held taut to direct it over the net. I like bumping into the guy with hair as gold as a Ken doll's. My team wins three times straight and the guy with gold hair asks me for my number. I give him an old number, from the apartment Mama and I lived in years ago. I wouldn't mind seeing him again. I wouldn't mind touching that gold hair of his. But all I need is Donald finding out. Donald would pitch a fit on my head.

When Donald gets back from Lac du Flambeau, he doesn't notice my suntan. He has brought back enough fish to fill our freezer and my mother's. I like opening the freezer door to look at all the blind-eyed fish stacked closely together. They remind me of the Bible story where Jesus feeds the masses with a few loaves of bread and a few fish. I have this crazy feeling our own supply will go on forever.

His first night back Donald holds me gently after we've gone to bed. His touch is so warm and light I begin to feel that no skin can separate us tonight. All the tiny particles scientists say scoot around to form our bodies have reorganized themselves. My quarks stir themselves up with Donald's, so in the span of only a few minutes we have become one person.

"You're all I've got," Donald murmurs. He is starting his warm-up dance in our bed. The covers roll off his hard, creased body. Rhythm is taking him over, making his hands shake.

"Lois," he says, and it is the best thing I have heard all night. "Lois," Donald whispers in the dark like he has just said he loves me.

~ ~

Donald ignores me when I finally start to show. He spends more time with his friends. Donald's two best friends, Edsel Fast Wolf and Glen Fredericks, are Sioux. They are two self-proclaimed good-time boys who beat it out of Rapid City, South Dakota, when they were just kids. The way Glen tells it, they left just in time.

"Whites in Rapid City feel about Ind'ins the way the KKK in Mississippi feels about blacks. You hear what I'm saying?"

"You know it . . ."

"You said it . . ."

Donald and Edsel back him up like they're a singing group.

Glen and Edsel come over on weekends, never during the week, because despite their big talk they are hard workers. Edsel is Inspector Number 76 at a cheese factory, and Glen is a lineman for the phone company.

All three of them use the same old lines when they drink. Today, as I'm washing the dishes, I catch myself mouthing their words along with them, under my breath: "Those Bulls are getting supernatural. They're going to take home seventy wins this season, you watch. Yeah, you mean if Dennis Rodman or Billy Laimbeer don't kill one of them first. Hey, I ever tell you about that little Navajo girl with the wood leg?"

Some people can learn plays by heart or recite poetry. I can regurgitate these bonding sessions like a tape recorder.

From behind I can't tell Edsel and Glen apart. They both have shoulder-length brown hair drizzling down their backs into halfhearted split-end ponytails. Their hair is not thick and black like Donald's. I have never seen them without their beaded White Sox caps pulled down low over their eyes. They like to reminisce about Vietnam, or maybe they just have to.

"Hey, we were primed for Vietnam," Glen is saying, "because we had lifetime training. It's guerilla warfare in some of those little redneck towns." Glen squints into his bottle as he talks. He has a big dimple in his left cheek that makes it look like he's smiling all the time. Edsel is the quiet one. His fine, large hands rest comfortably on his thighs, and he nods his head at whatever Glen is saying. Every now and then he strokes the hairs on his upper lip with an index finger. That scraggly mustache has been a work-in-progress for as long as I've known him.

When Donald is with Glen and Edsel he forgets he

never made it past boot camp. All of a sudden he was there beside them when they shipped out, he took a bullet for Edsel, he carried Glen on his back to a chopper under fire. He is one fierce Rambo warrior with a steel plate that resonates when he toasts a beer bottle against his thigh.

As usual, they forget I'm there. So I go in the bedroom to work on my secret beadwork. I'm trying to finish one of my favorite pieces, which I've been beading for two months. It pictures Glen, Edsel, and Donald together in Vietnam, just like Donald's fantasy. They are in a dry, yellow field; the brittle grass is gold like cornsilk. They're wounded and waiting for help. Donald is between Glen and Edsel with his arms around their shoulders. They are all looking up at the sky.

I used to think I had control over the scenes I create, but now I'm not so sure. I hate the way they are so alone in the picture, but I can't seem to change anything. If I stare at it for too long as a whole piece, I start to cry because I know what my needle won't let me stitch. Hope.

"You're my brother."

"You are my brother."

Voices from the living room curl under the bedroom door, and I open it a crack to peek at the men. The friends have hit the weeping stage and are close to passing out. They punch each other's arms, their heavy turquoise rings leaving bruised circles.

"I love you, man."

"No, I love you."

"I love both of you."

Their overlapping words are a round song. No one hears them but me.

～～

I'm six months pregnant and can hold the baby in my cupped hands. Sometimes its feet press against my palms, pushing off them like they're a springboard at the YMCA pool. Me and the baby go over to Mama's for breakfast, the same as always.

Mama is on the floor of her bedroom, still in her baby doll nightgown and large hair rollers. It suddenly occurs to me that I don't know the true color of Mama's hair. She and Lady Clairol are tight; Mama changes hair color the way other people change clothes. I don't know why she bothers to roll her hair over fat pink sponges, since she teases it into one of those tired old beehive hairdos every day of her life.

Mama nails me with her speckled green eyes. "Look what I got here." She points to papers strewn on the floor, stranding her on a small island of carpet. "Did you know I kept all your report cards?"

I shrug. Me and the baby sit down on her unmade bed and I flip through *TV Guide*. I hope Phil Donahue has a really hot show today, like the ex-wives of celebrities dishing the dirt. I like the way they carry on and talk about how five thousand dollars a month alimony is chicken feed.

"You were a good student. Look at this. Come *here.*" Mama pulls me down on the floor, into her atmosphere of White Shoulders perfume. She keeps thrusting report cards in my face, one after the other, going all the way back to kindergarten.

"So?"

"*So?* You got a B+ in your civics speech class and all you can say is, *So?* What I'm saying is, you've still got avenues. You should finish high school, maybe go to night school, and I could watch the baby. Or—"

I'm trying to cut in, but she slices the air with her hand like she's dicing onions.

"—Or you could just study at home for the G.E.D. One way or the other. It would be criminal not to get your diploma. Just criminal."

"You never got yours," I tell her. And she looks pretty much alive to me, sitting there in her emerald-colored baby doll nightgown that really brings out the green of her eyes.

"There," she says, satisfied. "You've just made my whole case. Why would you want to do like I did? I'd swap with you in a second to get another chance."

"What about Donald?" I ask her. I'm used to Donald being the last word.

"What *about* him? He's got fourteen years on you, but he's the child. For the life of me, I don't see what the big attraction is. What do you like about him?"

Mama thinks she's got me. She thinks I'm quiet because I can't come up with a single example. But the truth is, I don't know where to start. The truth is also that some of the things I'd like to tell her would sound silly. When Donald isn't drunk his eyes are soft, like brown soil. He has great big hands that look as if they hurt him because the skin is stretched so tight over knotted knuckles, his fingers pumped too full of blood. He had these special tattoos made on his knuckles. He said he got the idea from an old Robert Mitchum movie, *Night of the Hunter.* One hand has *LOVE* written across the knuckles, and the other spells out *HATE.* He can do the whole monologue Robert Mitchum did in the movie about the struggle between love and hate, and when Donald finishes he always cries, drunk or sober.

I have three pockmarks on my forehead from when I had the chicken pox as a baby. Donald uses his pinkie finger to trace them into a triangle. He calls it "The Bermuda Triangle."

"I got lost in here," he whispers in my ear. "I met you and just got lost. Went overboard. This is where you keep your tricky love spells, huh?"

Donald is the cleanest person I know. He says it goes

back to the military. Donald is maybe the only man on this earth who can go on a three-day drunk where he can't even tell you his name, and still shower, shave, and splash on some Old Spice before staggering back to the scene of the crime.

"Donald never forgets an anniversary. He gets me flowers every time," is what I finally tell Mama.

"Oh? And he probably gets you flowers after beating the crap out of you, too?" Mama looks like she wants to slap me. I even flinch, but instead she pulls me into the meanest, hardest hug I've ever had. We're kneeling on the report cards. I'm watching my tears fall on the fourth grade card with its crawling As and Bs; my tears are smudging them until they look like a foreign alphabet, or maybe some of those Chinese characters.

"If I can't make you see that you have choices," Mama sobs, "I'm going to go crazy!"

Mama releases me suddenly and me and the baby lurch sideways onto the carpet. Mama scuttles to the bed on her knees, shoving her hand under the bed like she's grabbing for the tail end of a cat. She pulls out the Cool Whip bowl with Dad's ashes inside. Mama sits cross-legged in front of me. She has pretty, slim legs. I guess she's not an old lady yet.

Mama doesn't remove the lid, but taps it sharply with a bloodred fingernail. "This dead S.O.B. sold me a line, and I bought it. I bought his whole worldview for cry sakes. They didn't have these talk shows and magazine articles back then about what you could expect from a man. You hear that? What *you* can *expect.* You've got to want something for yourself," she tells me. "You deserve to get something."

"I'll have the baby," I tell my mother. And me and the baby go home.

~ ~

It's a week before Christmas and the baby is due any day now. It can pop out at any second. Donald was drinking eggnog while we watched the Dr. Seuss special *How the Grinch Stole Christmas,* but now he is drinking something stronger and is starting to look like the Grinch himself.

"Kids' stories always cop out at the end," he is telling me. "What does that teach a kid? I come from a big family, and one after the other we all learned that this happy ending garbage is just a lot of bullshit."

"I don't know, Donald. You're too profound for me," Mama says and winks at me. Donald ignores her and her remarks, which is fine with me. I don't want a fight.

"You take those Whos down in Whoville," Donald continues, pulling me closer to him so he can be sure I'm paying attention. "Look like goddamn furry roaches, don't they? If they were so happy without all their Christmas shit—gifts and toys and food and decorations—then the Grinch should've just kept it. That'd teach little kids something. That'd give them some real values. Some kids won't get anything, just like we didn't. But a story like that would prepare them."

Mama yawns and rises from the couch. She kisses me good-bye. "I think I'll take off. This is getting too heavy for me," she tells Donald and leaves.

"What does your mother know?" Donald asks me. I shrug. I want to tell him that I don't know anything myself. The closer I get to having the baby, the less I remember. Yesterday I spent an hour trying to get through the times tables up to twelve, and when I couldn't even get past the threes, I just sat there crying. Maybe I know less and less because the baby knows more and more? What if this is a genius baby?

I know I'll have a nightmare about it tonight. Something horrible like I give birth to a talking baby. It talks just like Donald, swearing at me from the moment the doctor slaps it on the butt. Then it looks at me, hanging upside down in the doctor's hands. At first I think it's the spitting image of Donald, right down to those LOVE and HATE tattoos stenciled on its tiny fists. But then I see its eyes. They aren't warm like brown soil. They are black and empty like little watermelon seeds.

Donald is thoroughly drunk now. His nose is as red as that reindeer's they sing about on the radio. He is getting so angry his forehead is sweating.

"So, where is it?!" he yells at me all of a sudden. I back up against the TV set. I haven't sat down once all evening because if I do, I'll be stranded. I can't trust Donald to help me up again.

"Where is what?"

"That DOOMED kid of ours!"

"Don't say that. It isn't doomed." Static makes my blouse stick to the television screen. Maybe that's what gives me this suicidal courage to face Donald. Maybe I'm not real, just another character looking out of the TV. Donald is on his feet now.

"What else do you call a kid nobody wants?"

"DON'T LET IT HEAR!" That's the first time I've ever yelled at Donald and my throat burns. I'm waiting for Donald to do something. I'm waiting for his hand to twist in my hair or peel the skin off my face, or at least for his voice to spray hot words like all those crazy rounds of bullets on *Miami Vice*. Donald just stands there, tense and awkward, until our breath is pressing us against the walls.

"You thought of any names yet?" he whispers, cracking the knuckles of his right hand.

"No," I breathe, and it's safe now to take a few steps closer to him.

"Figures," he mutters, and turns around in one twist of the heel. He knocks his knuckles against the wall on his way out of the apartment without looking at me. He slams the door, but I don't hear him going down the stairs. When I peek out of the peephole in the door I can see that he is still standing there, right outside, so close to the door his magnified head curves and hovers before my eyes like a black planet.

Donald is subdued and won't give me any more trouble tonight, but I can't relax. Now the baby is mad. It's heavier than it was a half hour ago because it is sulking. Donald is still motionless in the hallway when his child, unnamed and unborn, balls up its tiny hands into fists and begins pounding me from the inside.

Angry Fish

The day I met Saint Jude I was thinking impure thoughts about Lena Catches, the one I called *Sinihimaniwinga*—Cold Walking Woman. I was visiting her resale shop, known as Lena's Second Chance, as I did every morning, bringing her one sugar donut and one chaste kiss. I was hoping that the kiss would reach her lips one day, but she was quick; when she saw me moving toward her she tucked her lips in her mouth and thrust one round cheek forward to receive a dry peck. I wanted to tell her that my sandpaper lips would soften to velvet and my mouth would taste like cream if she'd just let down her old lady hair and dust the prim particles off her body. But I thought maybe a confession like that would set me back.

I was taught that it's bad manners to walk with hands in your pockets, but watching Lena, I had to plunge mine in the fabric to keep them still. My fingers wanted to comb through her hair, smudge her face powder, work the zippers and buttons of her confining clothes like little locks to her rooms. Lena always wore pantsuits that were the soft colors of baby clothes. She liked everything to match: her shoes, handbag, eye makeup, even the plastic headband she wore in her hair. She was in her late sixties by then, but her face was unwrinkled, and she rinsed her hair a deep blue black.

"Lena, you are too perfect," I teased her that morning.

"What's that?" She was reading the *National Enquirer.*

"You're perfumed, sprayed, and ironed like those Miss America girls. Spit and polish. I'm waiting for a rainstorm and then you better look out. I'm going to soak you in the rain!"

Lena licked the tip of her finger to turn the page. She wasn't listening. It was just as well because I knew the rain would have more sense than to drench Lena Catches. Even if I carried her out to the street in the middle of a storm I imagined the rain would slide harmlessly off her body as if her skin were not porous, as if her clothes were made of sheet metal.

"Listen to this one, Mitchell," she said. "In a small town near Albuquerque three humanoid aliens interrupted a third grade class to take the children's blood pressure. Here's the quote: 'Mrs. Daily told our reporter that she and her students were in a hypnotic trance. They cooperated fully with the intruders and made no attempts to flee. The aliens were friendly and appeared to communicate through a complicated system of humming. Their medical instruments were unremarkable, possibly borrowed from a local hospital. The visit lasted approximately forty-five minutes.'"

Lena sighed and cut the article out of the paper to include in her UFO scrapbook. I knew that later she would use a red pen to plot the sighting in her *Rand McNally Road Atlas*. States such as Utah and Wyoming were peppered with red dots, even southern Illinois was lightly sprinkled, but so far there weren't any sightings plotted in our Chicago area.

"There are hot spots," Lena told me the first time I noticed her special road atlas. "I can't tell you *why,* but I can see a pattern. I'm saving my money and any day now I'll head for one of those active places. It's just a matter of being in the right place at the right time."

Lena had a one-track mind when it came to UFOs and aliens from outer space. I could pick any topic of conversation and she would shift the subject to another sighting, or the discovery of another galaxy. I could understand her single-minded interest. I saw the way it filled her up and kept her mind busy, tumbling and whirring in a way that was healthy. When her husband died of cancer, she hadn't retreated into the bitter arena of memories and regrets, but had secured a small loan from the American Indian Businessman's Association to open her shop. Safely installed amidst her musty merchandise, she had begun to contemplate all the worlds shining beyond our vision.

Lena put down her scissors and returned to the

National Enquirer. I liked to watch her read. Her round Oneida face puckered in concentration and her pale green eyes—the color of creamy jade—attacked the page as if the act of reading made her angry. It reminded me of the way my father had read newspapers, clenching the paper so tightly in his fists his knuckles turned white. Reading was difficult for him, despite his education at the Carlisle Indian School in Pennsylvania, because Winnebago was his first language. He didn't like to think in English.

"English looks at the world this way," he told me, cutting the air with a flat chop parallel to the ground. *"Hocunkgara* sees the world like this." His hand moved in a circle.

~ ~

My father and my Sioux mother had met at Carlisle but didn't remain there after graduation.

"They taught us to be white," my father told me when I was still too young to understand. "They taught us that way but didn't give us anywhere to take it." He slapped his hands together and fine dust emerged from his flesh; clouds burst from his palms.

"And I'm glad," he whispered, kneeling so his lips grazed my ear. "I'm back in the world now."

We lived near Green Bay in Wisconsin, where my father spent his days tending our small orderly fields of corn, squash, and beans, and his nights deep in the

woods at secret medicine lodge meetings. When he
returned, I could smell cedar on his clothes, his hair
smoky. His scent filled our three rooms like pungent
incense.

"You're like a church," my mother told him once,
laughing.

I fell asleep to the sound of his voice. It scratched
the walls and windows, raw from his prayers and sacred
songs. He discussed clan politics with my mother, but
I never digested the details. I was too transfixed by the
strained quality of his voice. *My father really knows how to
pray,* I thought.

My father's hands were hallowed, unlike mine, which
have been soiled by steel. I saw him bend flexible reeds
into animal figures: dogs, rabbits, hawks. When he
breathed on the figure's face it would come to life for
several moments and behave like any other of its kind.
The hawk would coast above our heads and the dog rub
against my legs. But eventually the creature would come
apart, break open to reveal a nest of weeds.

I left Wisconsin because my parents barely scratched
out a living from their few crops. I figured I could find
a good job in the city and send home half my wages. It
was just after World War II, and the government was
pushing Relocation, moving Indians from reservations
into the cities. Like many other Indians, I went into construction. We liked to work on high-rise buildings, weav-
ing steel girders into solid structures that pierced the

sky. We were careless on the catwalks and strolled exposed beams twenty stories high as casually as if we were on the ground. I am at least partially responsible for that Lake Michigan skyline. I thought I was bringing something to life back then, but after my parents died, I wasn't so sure. They succumbed to a virulent flu sweeping the Midwest, and I wondered where they would go. I couldn't see them following their teachers into Christ's jeweled heaven. They would be as uncomfortable there as they'd been at Carlisle.

I stayed in construction, but at night I practiced writing, trying to plot my place in the world as neatly as Lena Catches plotted close encounters on her maps. I wrote a poem for my father that was published twenty years later in *Akwesasne Notes*. This is what I told him on the page:

> *My father is heretic pine,*
> *his ashes grown to needles in Wisconsin woods.*
> *I visited the grave and found him*
> *risen in bark.*
> *I smeared his heart's sap on my fingers.*
> *He will not wash away.*
> *I found God speaking Winnebago,*
> *perched in a silver birch tree.*
> *Tiny birds covered him like a feathered quilt.*
> *He was chewing fronds of fern*
> *to keep his teeth sharp and white.*
> *I saw him tremble like a bear,*

freeze like a deer,
withdraw like a turtle into his shiny bones.
Winnebago God blessed me from the tree.
His fists rang on either side of my head
where he shook them like rattles.
City brother, he teased,
welcome to this old universe.

～ ～

I lived in the uptown area near the Chicago Indian
Center, which was where I met Lena and her husband,
Ray Catches. I didn't covet her then. It wasn't until Ray
died that I noticed her little mouth and striking green
eyes. In the five years since my retirement, Lena and I
had established a pattern: she ducked my kisses and
ate my donuts. In the back room of her shop I sorted
through boxes of donated items, separating worthless
contents from more promising discards while Lena read
the tabloids. Once the contents were sorted, Lena made
an inventory list and assigned prices. Sometimes I came
across items we squirreled away for ourselves. Lena took
possession of pastel pantsuits, leather purses, and science fiction magazines, while I kept a backgammon set
and a huge macrame tapestry of an owl with startled
eyes large as dinner plates.

～ ～

The day I discovered Saint Jude—or, as some may prefer to think, he discovered me—I was pawing through a box of business suits which had been worn to a shine. Five unopened boxes were stacked behind me. I was checking the pockets of each suit jacket for money or other valuables when I heard a scraping sound. A box behind me rattled, shook, threatened to fall from the top of the stack. *Somebody probably dumped their pet,* I was thinking as I moved to open the box. It contained cookingware: pots and pans once coated with teflon, plastic spatulas burned into unusual shapes, hand mixers, a garlic press, and underneath the clutter, the lumpy plastic statue of a saint.

"Hey, you," the statue hissed. I would have dropped him back into the box, but his tiny hands caught my sleeve and he dangled from the cuff of my shirt.

"I'm talking to you," the voice continued. "Don't you dare put me back in that box!"

"You can talk," I said stupidly. The figure rolled his eyes and knocked his head against one arm to right the halo, which had slipped down on his forehead.

"Funny how I can converse more capably when I'm not hanging in space."

I quickly caught the plastic saint by the waist, but I must have squeezed too hard because I knocked the breath from his molded body. Finally he pointed to a worktable and I set him down.

"This is not an auspicious introduction," he complained.

I was becoming annoyed with his petulance. "So, who's been introduced?"

The saint smoothed his robes and adjusted his halo. "I am Jude, martyr of my faith. Executed by order of Nero Domitius, fifth emperor of Rome, enemy of the Christian world. Who are you?"

For a moment I thought maybe I had breathed life into this statue the way my father had animated straw. But he was too lively. He scraped his sandaled feet against the pedestal; he bent to scratch his knee.

I finally answered, "I'm Mitchell Black Deer. Half Winnebago and half Sioux. Deer clan on my father's side. Originally from Wisconsin."

I decided I was dreaming. Maybe in bed. Maybe sitting at the worktable in Lena's shop with my head in my arms.

"Deer clan?" The saint shook his head. "We are all of the fish clan, little brother. We are all children of the Holy Fisherman." He held out his small hands and I noticed the outline of a fish traced in each palm.

"Do you want to kiss the hem of my robe?" he asked.

"No," I replied. Jude shrugged his shoulders and picked at the frayed ends of his rope belt. I didn't mean to be rude, but I would not bow my head before his white robe. I would not worship his small white toes and stringy hair. However, I *did* agree to take him home with me when he begged. I offered to pay Lena for the statue, although I didn't mention that he'd spoken to me just moments earlier in the back room.

"Since when did you get religion?" she asked. She sounded suspicious.

"Oh, no. He's just for decoration. A little irony," I lied.

She wouldn't accept any money for the statue. "He hasn't even been painted," she pointed out. It was true. He was pure white, smudged here and there by dirty fingerprints. I carried him out of the store, and because I thought I was dreaming I didn't worry about the unopened boxes I'd left behind, which would be extra work for Lena.

It was well into the night before I decided I was awake. It was a sharply cold October evening and I'd opened the windows in my apartment, hoping to rouse myself. I began to shiver and even the saint quivered on the coffee table.

"You're real," I finally admitted, closing the windows and turning up the thermostat. Jude snapped his eyes. "Why did you come to *me?*" I sat before him on the couch.

"You opened the box. You were just in the right place at the right time. And I'm glad you've come to your senses, because I need your help."

I waited for him to continue.

"I want to write poems," Jude told me. "I need someone to transcribe my poems for posterity. Maybe put together a little chapbook."

He discussed the themes and ideas he planned to ar-
ticulate. He had no desire to be appended to the Bible,
and it was my impression that this was because his words
might be critical of the regime; the complex government
of spirit in the Christian afterlife, he said, was strictly
hierarchal.

"The cliques, the jealousy," he muttered. "Issues
of seniority. Who was canonized first. Whose miracles
were more imaginative. Those who died a martyr's
death versus those who died in their sleep. It's endless.
Then, too, today's faithful are barely making it to the
celestial level. Standards have been lowered. No one's
celibate. No one's taken a vow of poverty. Half the
clergy are agnostic and when you try to provide them
with concrete evidence, such as a direct visitation, they
appeal to psychiatrists."

Jude threw his hands in the air and I wagged my head
politely in sympathy.

$\sim\sim$

Within a week Saint Jude and I settled into a routine.
In the morning he would compose poetry I carefully
tapped out on an ancient manual typewriter given to

me by my father. He stuttered sometimes, fumbled for the precise word. He had me consult the dictionary time and again, listening with eyes closed to the definitions I read aloud. Jude was critical of his own work. Perhaps one in ten poems would be acceptable. In the afternoon we edited the day's output, and in the evenings Jude meditated while I played Lakota language tapes. I had grown up speaking Winnebago and was now attempting to learn my mother's language.

I don't think Jude realized that he was learning Lakota as well. The tapes played in the background and I often heard him repeat phrases in the measured tone of a mantra:

"*Wicahpi owinza kin lila waste.* The star quilt is very pretty."

"*Wacipi ekta ni kta he?* Are you going to the powwow?"

"*Pispiza kin wanlaka he?* Did you see the prairie dog?"

I never saw Jude sleep or eat, although I offered him whatever I was having. One evening I cooked corn soup and he sniffed the air in a pitiful way.

"Are you hungry?" I asked him.

"I don't need your kind of sustenance," he said, "but I do enjoy the cooking aroma."

"Let's fill you up then." I held Jude over my cast-iron soup kettle. The broth sparkled like liquid gold and its steam warmed our faces. Jude inhaled the cooking breath of corn and venison until his cheeks grew fat.

He flapped the long sleeves of his robe to capture more of the steam.

"This is good," he sighed, squirming in my hands like a white bird trying to fly into the soup. "This is so good!" He grew heavy, and when I placed him on the coffee table beside my plate, he loosened his rope belt.

～ ～

I was too busy attending to Jude to worry about Lena. I wasn't sure she would even notice my absence. But two weeks after I brought Jude home, she came by to check on me. She'd never visited my place before, and I think she was surprised at how small it was. I lived in a furnished efficiency, and my kitchen was little more than a closet with burners and a sink. I had taken the owl tapestry off the wall because Jude said it unnerved him, so the walls were bare when Lena entered. She carried a shopping bag full of plastic containers. When she unpacked them in my tiny kitchen I saw she had brought me starchy dishes I associated with Winnebago wakes and feasts: fry bread, potato salad, hominy, and grits.

"Are you sick?" she asked me. For a moment I thought she would check my forehead for a temperature. I shook my head, no.

"You should have a telephone," she scolded. "In case of emergencies."

I invited her to share supper with me, the supper she had cooked, but she waved the offer away with her hand.

"I can't stay long. I was just worried about you when you didn't show. I thought maybe aliens had spirited you away, and here I missed it."

She smiled, and I realized it was the first time she'd ever poked fun at her obsession. I noticed that her face was no longer smooth as the porcelain doorknob to my closet, but delicately wrinkled, and silver white strands sprouted from her hairline like a glistening spiderweb combed into her hair. I thought she had never been more beautiful.

"Lena Catches," I murmured, taking her hand in mine. "I have some business to finish, but then I'll turn up again. I'll be seeing you all the time."

She blushed from her throat to the tips of her ears. At the door she put her arms around me and pressed her forehead to my breastbone. Just before pulling away, she tipped her head back and kissed my mouth. It was the light kiss of a young girl, and we laughed, because for one moment all our years fell from us like scales.

"Lena missed me," I told Jude. He sulked on the sink drainboard, watching me rinse ears of sweet corn. "Who would've thought it?"

Jude shook his head. "It never fails. A woman beckons, a man follows. From the beginning of time to the end of time. It's so predictable, it's depressing."

"You're jealous," I teased. I expected Jude to laugh.

Instead he ran a thumb along the edge of his halo as if testing a knife blade. It was a nervous tic I suspected signalled insecurity.

"Am not," he said.

For the first time since Jude caught my sleeve with his miniature hands, I thought to myself, *We have got a problem.* I never intended to give my life over to Saint Jude. I hadn't thought beyond the completion of his chapbook. Where would he go when the last poem was revised and typed? I was suddenly so preoccupied with Lena I knew there wouldn't be room for him when I courted her in earnest. He was too demanding, too exhausting.

The strategy I devised to prepare him for our eventual separation wasn't very kind. I harped on our cultural incompatibility. I told him his idea of heaven could never be mine. I told him I preferred God sitting in a birch tree chewing grass to God reclining on a golden throne. I showed him photographs of my ancestors: men in buckskin breeches wearing single eagle feathers rising from their deer tail headdresses, women with long silver earrings and thick strands of wampum around their necks wearing silk applique dresses.

"Have you seen them in your afterlife?" I asked him. He studied the pictures and shook his head sadly.

"I didn't think so. They're somewhere else. We are deer, bear, and elk clans, buffalo, water spirit, and warrior clans, but we are not your fish clan. We have never been your fish clan."

This is how I argued the night before Jude composed his last poem, the one I liked best. He called it "Angry Fish," and when I read it back to him he nodded and wiped his eyes.

"That's how I feel," he said. "That's the song of the martyrs."

It was a long poem, a kind of lament, but the last phrases lodged themselves in my brain so that I remember them even now:

> In the barrel of God's cupped palm
> the fish are angry.
> Their faith-hooked flesh
> cannot heal in the briny tears
> God shed for them too long ago.
> They are marred by their infirmities,
> fish with serrated scales and spiny ridges
> unable to press one against the other
> for comfort.
> Scraped raw by love,
> dipped in wax and held to the flame.
> Faith's cold fire chills the heart.

Saint Jude's manuscript included sixty poems and was eighty-five pages long. I held it for a time in my hands, appreciating its weight and the sharp scent of fresh pages. I packed it in a typing paper box that I bound with twine.

"It's done. Mission accomplished," I told Jude. He nodded, and blessed me with his tiny fingers.

～ ～

Four weeks after we first met, I returned Jude to his people. I wrapped him in a soft piece of buckskin, since it was cold that morning. I hadn't told him where I was taking him because I didn't want to argue. I'd bought a large Easter basket from Woolworth's—cheap, out of season—and wrapped a white ribbon around its handle. This is how I carried the manuscript, and Jude, straddling the box with the buckskin pulled around him like a blanket.

It was so quiet that morning I could hear stoplights change from red to green as I stood beneath them. I walked all the way to Saint Michael's Church, a longer walk than I'd managed in recent years—something like four miles. The rectory was in back; three wrought-iron steps led to the front door, and an elaborate bell was rigged above the entrance. I placed the basket on the top step, poised to ring the bell.

"Take care, old man," I whispered, but he wouldn't look at me. He seemed stiffer, his arms straight at his sides, his feet still. He stood on the manuscript and stared vacantly ahead, the flap of leather fallen around his ankles.

"This is where you really belong." I felt guilty, but it quickly turned to anger. I had played host long enough. I was tired of Indians playing host until we were pushed out of our own lives. But I didn't tell Saint Jude. I didn't want to hurt his feelings.

I rang the bell and stepped back. As I turned to go I heard a muffled voice. "Good-bye," Jude said. I moved down the steps, and he called, *"Unlowanpi,"* the Lakota phrase for, "We are singing together."

I passed through the courtyard and was on the street when I heard his lonely voice singing a song he must have learned from my powwow tapes. It told the story of two brothers reunited after a battle, delighted to discover that they have both survived. I took up the song while I could still hear Jude's voice and sang it, all the way home.

Wild Turnips

It must be a sign of getting old. I find I've put my feet somewhere. Perhaps I left them in my shoes, which are still tucked beneath my twin bed, but I don't see them poking out when I look. I don't see a swatch of ankle rising from the untied laces. My husband, Percy, was a foot man, so I always took good care of my feet. I used a pumice stone to grind away the calluses and creamed the soles every night. What would he say now? How can someone misplace her feet?

I ask the young attendant who looks something like my grandson. His hair is black with a streak of pink behind his left ear, but I don't mention the pink because it could be my eyes. They could be going rainbow on me.

I ask him, "Everett, have you seen my feet?"

Everett continues emptying the wastebaskets, mine and my roommate's, but he doesn't answer me. I touch his sleeve and ask him again.

"Huh?" He pulls off the headphones I should have noticed and wears them around his throat like a necklace.

"Everett, have you seen my feet?"

Everett points to a region below my knees. My feet are back. They are inside royal blue Isotoner slippers my *wasicun*, white, son-in-law Carl sent me.

~ ~

"I met my husband, Percy, at the Carlisle Indian School in Pennsylvania," I tell my roommate, Gertrude. She is cutting faces out of magazines like *Family Circle* and *Ladies' Home Journal,* pasting them on large white sheets of paper with rubber cement. The fumes make her silly, make her giggle into a lace hankie.

"They took both of us from our families when we were just little. I didn't see my parents for seventeen years."

Gertrude is pasting little faces on larger ones and a prone red dog in the right-hand corner of the page.

"Can you imagine?" I ask her.

"We had to lock him up," Gertrude tells me, suddenly sober. She reaches inside her sweater sleeve to yank out a withered pink tissue. She wipes her dentures and her mouth and replaces the tissue.

"George went loony in the winter of 1926, so little George and Peter locked him up in the barn. But he frightened all the horses so bad we ended up putting him in the root cellar."

There is one paper face Gertrude decides does not

belong with the others. She tries to pull it off, but the rubber cement stretches, oozing like mucus. When she gets the face off she crumples the face into a ball and stuffs it inside her sleeve.

"Why did he go loony?" I ask. I may be old, but I'm not so old as Gertrude. I can follow her conversation, even if mine slithers everywhere around her head but into her big wrinkled ears weighted by fake pearl earrings.

"I don't know," Gertrude says. She stops working and looks down at her hands. Her fingernails are cracked and ragged as if she has been clawing through dirt, and veins cross the backs of her hands like strands of blue yarn.

"I think it was all those blizzards," she finally tells me. "When the snow kept falling, making it white and whiter, until the whole world was white, he said he saw faces out there. Hundreds of faces." She dips her brush in the rubber cement.

That is the one thing I never understand about *wasicuns*—how they can go crazy out on the prairies. What is so bad, so frightening to them that their ideas jumble around like Ping-Pong balls in a bingo wheel? I could sit out on the prairies forever, never seeing anyone, and be happy. Then maybe I could remember all the things that keep slipping through the cracks. But I don't say any of this to Gertrude. I don't even ask her if George regained his senses because if he didn't, the memory of it will stay with her for days. Memories take me over just like that.

North Dakota is right outside our window, beyond the nursing home parking lot. I was already here when they poured the cement for that lot. Sometimes I think I should just walk through the automatic glass doors and get a good whiff of the sun. Maybe if I kept going and didn't once look back they wouldn't see me. I know if I could find a good pair of moccasins I would never get tired. I would get younger and younger as I traveled through our territory. I would follow the Grand River and listen for the ghost singers to tell me stories.

I have five Sioux daughters, but not one of them lives Indian Way. If they did, I would be living two months out of the year with each one in turn, and then two months back on the Standing Rock Reservation with some of my old friends who are still alive and kicking. But I am never angry with their choices or directions because when the time came I blew them from my hand the way you blow the seeds of a dandelion.

They pay for me to stay in this place where I am the only Sioux, although there is one other Indian—an old Assiniboin man who calls me "Little Sister" and tells me I should set my beautiful long hair free of the heavy black hairnet the nurses catch it with each morning.

"And what would that do?" I ask him, reaching out to pinch the loose skin at his wrist.

"It would put me back," he says, straightening in his

wheelchair and looking over my shoulder right into the sun.

I think if you peeled him like a hard-boiled egg and found the green, smooth, sapling piece of him, that piece would unfold, stretch, and rise, and his whole life would start all over again. There is a beginning inside him, lodged with his middle-life and tangled with his last days. One long string winding around and around like a yo-yo's.

⌒ ⌒

Irma calls me. "We took Wade to his first powwow," she says. "You should have seen him dance traditional, Mama. He has the moves down just right."

I sent Wade a small round mirror set in a wood frame decorated with brass tacks to use when he dances. His steps should recall a proud male bird, preening and watching his reflection in a pool of water. I want to tell Irma that she went to powwows *before* she was born. I sat near the drum when I was carrying her and patted the soft mound of her with my hand, in time to the music. It is why she is such a good dancer and knows all the old songs. I didn't wait until her fifth birthday as she has done with Wade. But that is sour grapes, so I tell her to send me snapshots of Wade in his costume.

"Send me some dried turnips," I tell my daughter.

She laughs. "Mama, what're you going to do with

them? You can't eat them without your teeth, and the nurses tell me you still won't wear your dentures."

"I'll manage," I say, and I will. If I have to soak those turnips for a month I will taste them, because their wild flavor is a freedom cut away from me.

When I hang up the phone, I notice Percy sitting on the edge of Gertrude's bed. He's blowing gently on her forehead, but she sleeps like a stone, like a little stone at the bottom of a well. I know Percy is trying to make me jealous. He wants to stir me to anger so I will rise up and follow him into the next world where he has been living all alone.

"I know you miss me," I tell him, holding out my hand so he will leave my roommate be. "I miss you, too. But I want nature to take its course. It can't be long now."

Percy shakes his head and refuses my hand. He leaves the room and passes through Everett like one of those crazy sustained notes I hear running out of the boy's earphones. Everett looks up from his work, dust mopping the halls. Then he shakes himself and reapplies the mop to the floor.

Percy hasn't forgiven me for living. I could have gone out Sioux Way, the way he did. He willed himself to make the journey, just put himself to sleep when his body gave him trouble. But I wanted to kick some more, and so here I am. Losing track of the days and of my own appendages, which can wiggle away from me when I'm not looking.

I'm lonely now that Percy has gone and Gertrude is still rolling beneath the waters of her dreams.

～ ➤

The activities director is a peahen with bright eyes and a pinched mouth. I suddenly recall why I usually avoid group activities. She wants us to *Get in touch with our feelings.*

"It is never too late to start writing," she assures us. She darts around the room, distributing pens and paper. "We must start with the close at hand and branch out from there."

Is this English? She doesn't stress any particular word but delivers them slowly, dropping one at a time. Apparently we are either too deaf or too stupid for her to lecture naturally. I force myself to smile at her because my anger tastes too bitter on my tongue. She wants us to describe our rooms.

"Let me see them in your work," she insists. "Make them vivid. I mean. Real."

I know vivid, I am thinking. I notice that I write it down.

I KNOW VIVID.

I am old, but I remember *vivid,* and it is *not* the same as *real.* (But that I don't write.) And maybe God is telling me, "Old woman, you do not know everything. You do not even know one hair on the head of everything, or one particle of dust on one hair on the head of everything. I'm going to show you your confusion."

I could believe God said that to me to teach humility and patience, because now I have the white paper on the table before me and the black pen in my hand, and I cannot see my room. I know there are beds, so I write, TWO BEDS. And a window, so I put down, ONE WINDOW. I make a list. But I am color-blind to my living quarters now. I cannot remember the decorations or feel the room's depth. I don't know if the floor is cold or the ceiling is high. Do we have curtains or blinds? Did my daughters send me any photographs?

I remember to put my roommate down. I write, ONE OLD GERMAN LADY, because with the pen in my hand I cannot even recall her name.

~ ~

One day the radios in this place are all lying. There are wagging pink tongues and dry lips behind every dial, telling the same story. I hear more and more about a President Bush.

"Who is this President Bush?" I ask Everett.

"Huh?" Everett pulls off his headphones.

"What about this President Bush?" I say again. "Who is he?"

"He's the new U.S. president," Everett says, replacing his music.

Then I know. This place is where they put the troublemakers, the radicals, the people who led delegations from their reservation to Washington, D.C., like I did. They must have a thick folder on each of us that they keep locked up, just like they keep us locked in here to stifle our protests. Maybe Gertrude is an old socialist who devoted her life to politics after her husband went loony.

How do I know all this? Because they cannot fool me. The president is Franklin Delano Roosevelt, and I have hopes for him yet. I know he will never let the Bureau of Indian Affairs push through the Indian Reorganization Act, placing puppet leaders in powerful tribal government positions. They are trying to cut us off from the true president and make us think there's another *wasicun* in charge.

It's never too late to start writing, I remember. They told us that in here. They let it slip. I take up my pen, which Gertrude stuffed inside her sleeve, reach over and slide it into my hand when she is dozing.

I write to President Roosevelt that Indians respect him, but we are not his children. We have never been the small children of *wasicun*s. I write such a long letter I get a cramp in my hand that spreads and burns along toward my elbow. I don't trust the activities director or any of the nurses to mail it for me. I send it to Irma, asking her to forward it.

~ ~

"Mama, I got your letter." Irma has a cold and keeps putting the phone down so she can blow her nose. I sent her muskrat roots to chew on, but she says they taste funny.

I can see her just as clear as if she were standing in my room. She has the phone pinned between her neck and shoulder, and she is using her free hands to fluff her short hair so it will have body by the time Carl gets home. She cut her hair off because she said it was so heavy it gave her headaches, and now she has to drive two hundred miles into Bismarck to get her hair permed by an Asian lady who "understands" Indian hair.

"Mama, President Roosevelt is dead. He died over forty years ago."

"Why are you trying to keep me quiet?" I ask her. I am sad. How can she see the last vestiges of tribal power siphoned away by locust bureaucrats? How can she see us reorganized? It is like being reformed or remade. How can she be in on this plot?

"I'm not trying to keep you quiet. I'm trying to level with you. You always say we treat you like a child, so Mama, I'm talking to you as an adult. Sometimes you lose track of time. President Roosevelt is dead. There have been nine presidents since him. You lived through it, you voted for some of them, but now you've blocked it out. That's the truth, Mom."

When my daughters call me "Mom," they are not Sioux. It is the other side they learned at school coming out. The little be-like-everybody-else animal stinking up our conversation.

"I believe you," I tell Irma, because she is not the smartest of my daughters, and maybe they have fooled her. I can fight this last battle on my own. I blew my daughters from my hand when it was time.

~ ~

I wake up with the red sun. Gertrude is snoring and her two skinny yellowed braids run straight up the pillow like antennae. I sit looking out of the window, but I must be getting powerfully old because I have misplaced the parking lot. It has always been white concrete painted with yellow lines tucked against this side of the building. It is gone. I can only see the hills that drove Gertrude's husband, George, mad. They roll away from me and wave. The grasses are cool green water.

Someone must have peeled me like an egg, pulled out the beginning.

I have yet to meet my first wasicun. *I do not speak English, only Dakota. I see a young buffalo calf trying to keep up with the herd, but he tumbles down one of the high green hills. The*

*calf becomes a pet and follows me everywhere. I sit quietly in
the tall prairie grass and watch birds flutter and strut, preening
themselves with a disdainful arrogance. I let my hair fall loose,
blown different ways by different winds. I gnaw a dried turnip
that tastes wild and bitter. I reach back for the old lady and
help her settle in the grass. I hold out the flat palm of my hand.
It is small and soft. When the old lady places her hand on top
of mine we laugh together, making one sound.*

*Then we lie back in the thick grass to watch the red sun be-
come the day sun.*

Beaded Soles

I am beading moccasins for my husband, Marshall
Azure. I am beading the soles so he can walk clear up to
the sky. There was a fuss about letting me have a needle.
They take it away at night so I can't use it as a weapon
to put out someone's eye.

The Chicago Indian Center took up a collection for
me to get whatever I needed, and I asked for cut beads,
sinew, and buckskin so I could make a pair of death
moccasins for Marshall to wear into the next world.

They're taking his body home to Fort Yates, North
Dakota, on the Standing Rock Sioux Reservation. I
won't be able to attend the services. It's just as well
though, because I know Father Zimmer's "Sermon for
a Dead Indian" by heart. He likes to call heaven "The
Happy Hunting Ground," but it is an Anglo heaven
Father Zimmer describes. It sounds like a great bureaucracy: the most sophisticated filing system in the
world, where all your sins and virtues are entered like
tax statements to the IRS. Father Zimmer's heaven is

exclusive—don't call us, we'll call you. Half the fun of being there is knowing others didn't make it.

Father's eyes change from blue to gray when he talks about heaven. His sharp overbite slices the words as they leave his mouth until he resembles a great snapping turtle rending pieces of flesh. He doesn't realize that later Herod Small War will negate him. Herod will clean Father's words from the congregation's mind. He will talk over the body of Marshall Azure in Dakota, and Father Zimmer will nod as though he understands. Herod will explain to Marshall that Indian heaven is democratic, it is home, it is the place where we shall all meet again to join in the Great Powwow which goes on well into the night. In Indian heaven the Dakota people wear moccasins with beaded soles and dance on air. Herod will tell Marshall to look for us later on, to meet us on the road when it is our turn to make the journey.

Even *I* will make it to Indian heaven, where I will dance all night with my husband, Marshall Azure, carrying our son, Jasper, in my arms.

$\sim\quad\sim$

On the reservation, memory is a sap that runs thick and deep in the blood. The community memory is long, preserving ancient jealousies, enmities, and alliances until they become traditional. In my family, memory was a soldier's navy blue tunic, stiffened on the left side with a spatter of sacred brown blood. Memory lured me into my parents' bedroom closet, where the tunic was kept on a hanger, covered by a flour sack.

My fingers unpinned the bottom of the flour sack to stroke the coarse material. I touched memory and pain in the dark back of the closet, biting the tip of my tongue and slowing my breath to its most silent. When I refolded the hem of the flour sack and repinned the garment, I wanted to leave memory behind me. My parents' bedroom closet should have been its museum. But memory's shadow pinned my own to the ground until some days I imagined I could feel God's thumb pressing on the crown of my head.

The soldier's tunic belonged to my great-grandfather, Lieutenant Henry Bullhead, an Indian policeman sent to arrest Sitting Bull. Lieutenant Bullhead was shot in the side by Catch-the-Bear—one of Sitting Bull's followers—and the lieutenant shot Sitting Bull as he fell. It was said that the soldier's wound wasn't serious, that he would have lived if Sitting Bull hadn't been fatally shot and fallen across him. The holy man's blood was enough to kill his enemy. Lieutenant Bullhead's blood washed away as Sitting Bull's blood drenched the policeman's jacket, poisoning his wound.

As it turned out, Lieutenant Bullhead got off easy. He died and his body was taken back to his family. They buried him dressed in a fresh uniform, his hands folded across his chest like a white man.

Lieutenant Bullhead left his sin behind him, scraped from his soul the way caked dirt had been knocked off his boots. The sin was left to his children.

~ ~

My great-grandfather's sin against our own tribe came down through the generations as if it was packaged in our genes. When a Bullhead made a misstep in life people would say, "What can you expect from a Bullhead?" Our word was doubted and we were considered unlucky. This last was true.

My father owned a horse we called *Ista Sa,* Red Eyes, for the angry glowing eyes in his black face. No one could safely approach *Ista Sa* except for my father, yet every morning the horse's mane and tail were plaited in tight knots, which my father spent a half hour untangling. It was said that mischievous *heyoka* spirits the size of small children played tricks on the dangerous horse to tease my father.

My mother never had success with her canning. No matter how careful she was, the chokecherry jelly would ferment and the tomatoes spoil until the mason jars exploded.

Our cabin burned to the ground in 1939, when I was nine years old, and the next year my father was killed by a bolt of lightning. He had just been paid for helping a white rancher break in a herd of wild ponies. He was found by the side of the road leading to the reservation, five silver dollars in each hand. My mother tried to give me one of the silver dollars so I would have something of my father's, but I wouldn't touch it. I imagined the scorched silver was evil.

My mother had always been generous, but after my father's death she gave away anything she considered frivolous. People trained themselves not to compliment her clothes, house, or vegetable garden because whatever they admired she would offer. I had been in Father Zimmer's catechism class long enough to believe she was doing penance. I finally asked her, when our small house was nearly empty.

"*Ina,*" mother, "are we repenting?" My mother was busy altering a dress for the wife of Mr. Mitchell, the reservation agent. We didn't own a sewing machine but her stitches were neatly uniform. She looked up from a flounced skirt.

"I don't understand," she said impatiently. She needed to finish the dress, which was to be worn that evening.

"Giving everything away. The blankets even."

"You're Dakota," she scolded. "I thought I raised you to be generous."

"But almost everyone else has more than us now."

"Greedy. Do we have to be like everyone else?" She was dismissing me. "Do you think we're like everyone else?"

No, I had never thought that. But perhaps we could have been. I never forgave my mother for marrying the grandson of Lieutenant Henry Bullhead. She could have chosen wisely. She'd had her pick of any Sioux, Cheyenne, or Assiniboin. My mother was a Sioux and French beauty, one of three Arshambault sisters who specialized in collecting hearts. And here she had chosen my father, taken his name, helped him create a child in his own image. She hadn't refused him the way I'd refused the silver dollar, not wanting what my father had to give me.

~ ~

My father was a tall, quiet man with a tremendously thick moustache. I secretly believed the heavy moustache was what kept him silent, making it too difficult for him to lift his upper lip.

I was an awkward version of my father, stretched to his height—nearly six feet tall—as a grown woman. People said I was like him, they called me handsome, but I felt too strong to be attractive. My hands and feet were too broad, my hair too thick. I could chop wood like a man and carry three times the load of kindling my mother carried.

People expected me to be an old maid. I had two strikes against me: being a Bullhead *and* physically powerful.

My mother tried to assure me. "Remember the Dakota War Women," she said. She reminded me about the Sioux women who chose to join their husbands in battle. "Your grandma killed this many of the enemy," my mother would say, holding up both hands to spread ten fingers. "She was one of the best fighters and everyone wanted her for a wife. The best thing is to fight side by side."

I almost smiled. I couldn't imagine my mother riding into the dirt and blood, her face painted black like a Sioux warrior. The songs of insult flung at the enemy would never sound mocking on her sweet tongue.

"Dakota men will respect you. They will value your strength," she promised.

Maybe Dakota men had seen too many movies in Bismarck. Movies where Jean Harlow pouted, Greta Garbo was silent, Merle Oberon fainted, and Claudette Colbert's eyes widened in innocent confusion. Either that or the long shadow of memory stretched across my face like a veil so I was hidden from consideration.

I was twenty years old before Marshall Azure came looking for me. He showed up on washing day, when my sleeves were rolled up and my arms looked long, like they extended forever. He came right up to me in back of our house, hands on his hips. When he looked me in the face our eyes were level.

"You remember me?" he asked, trying to puff himself

taller. I nodded, ready to crack down the middle with a huge smile.

"You're a Bullhead," he teased.

"You're a fathead." Words we had spoken before in the school yard of Saint Joseph's Catholic Indian School in Bismarck. The school had anticipated a showdown between us, the two tallest Dakotas in the third grade. Minnie, a Gros Ventre girl with a rapid tongue, spread the news when the time came. She must have seen it in our eyes.

We circled one another slowly, carefully balanced, working our toes into the ground. The first move wouldn't happen until we'd offered the words. We stood toe to toe, square-matched in height and frame like a reflection.

"You're a Bullhead," Marshall said, tapping me in the chest with a forefinger. There was a terrible pause. The children were delighted.

"You're a fathead." I spat, toed the dust so it kicked across his shins. We rolled on the ground, becoming dark earth, sometimes becoming one person. The struggle was even and lasted until Sisters Fatima and Michael pulled us apart. Blood was in Marshall's mouth, smearing his teeth. I felt a knot rising on my forehead. We smiled at one another, sudden allies.

For the rest of our school days we were conspirators. We whispered Sioux together in the halls and play yard, defiant of rules. We talked about the Sun Dance and Herod Small War, a powerful Yuwipi man. We wrote perfect essays the nuns tacked on the wall, and secret essays we passed back and forth through a great underground system of resistance. Essays on what it was to be Indian, what it was to refuse to forget.

Now Marshall Azure stood before me, a grown man. He was still restless in his own body, squirming a little in the sun. He had the pigeon-toes of a traditional dancer, and a straight Sioux nose so old-fashioned it was almost arrogant. His top lip lifted in a permanent sneer, reminding me of Kicking Bear, one of Sitting Bull's contemporaries. His skin was so even in its warm color I imagined old women had gone over it with their flat thumbs, smoothing and blending.

"I'm back," Marshall said, waiting. His silence pressed me to answer. I wanted to run my thumb across the plane of his forehead.

"Took you long enough," I answered, finally putting my arms around him in welcome.

⮜ ⮞

Marshall and I went down to Mobridge, South Dakota, to get married. We went to Happy Sam's place, about twenty miles out of town. Happy Sam was a white justice of the peace who specialized in Indian weddings. At powwows he handed out brochures that were so attractive most people on the reservation had one tacked on their cabin wall.

The cover pictured a handsome Sioux couple wrapped together in a star quilt. Their heads were bowed, the target of a pointing finger reaching down from a pulpit in the upper left-hand corner. Beneath the couple was printed:

HAS THE CHURCH RENOUNCED YOU?
DOES THE CHURCH STAND IN THE WAY
OF YOUR ETERNAL BLISS?

The following pages described how Happy Sam could make dreams come true. He married all comers—no questions asked.

We left the reservation and the state of North Dakota to get married because Marshall came from an important Sioux family.

"Your blood is from the Black Hills," his mother liked to say, exaggerating its purity. His family didn't want him linking his name to mine, marrying into the long shadows. But Marshall had a mind of his own.

Happy Sam was plucking a wild turkey when we pulled up. He was pasted with blood and feathers. He dropped his work and ran up to our car before we ever made a move to get out.

"You're *sure* you're going through with it?" he asked, wiping his hands on the seat of his overalls. "*And* you got the money?" Happy Sam hadn't smiled yet the way he did on the last page of the brochure. Marshall nodded. Happy Sam smiled. "I'll go wash up then," he said.

I watched him walk back toward his clean-painted two-story house. It was a soft blue that melted into the sky. I watched him climb the steps to his porch and open the front door. Just inside I could see a narrow hallway, the floor covered with an Oriental carpet runner. Happy Sam walked right across that runner in his blood-and-feathered clothes. I'd heard that he had Oriental rugs throughout the house in rich colors like wine red and royal blue. He had real Chantilly lace curtains at every window and tatted doilies on each piece of furniture.

Happy Sam's two sons appeared from somewhere behind the house. One carried an accordion and the other a fragile guitar that looked very old. They could have been twins, both about fifteen years old, all corners in their clothes, standing on long, skinny feet. Their hair was the shade of a match flame, silver white at the roots burning yellow at the tips.

They leaned against the house and stared at us, passive as two cows in a pasture. The accordion made me remember that back in the thirties Happy Sam had toured throughout the Dakotas with Lawrence Welk's band. He must have passed the music on to his sons.

When Happy Sam returned he was dressed in a worn black suit that had a plum purple shine in the sun. He wore black-and-red striped moccasins on his feet and a warbonnet on his head with feathers trailing all the way down his back to brush against the ground.

He motioned for us to stand beside him in front of the house. I realized then that we would be married outside, like every other Indian couple he led to eternal bliss. I'd heard that when it rained or snowed he would move as far as the porch, but that an Indian had never set foot on his Oriental rugs or sat on a piece of his doily-covered furniture. Somehow I had imagined that Marshall and I would be exceptions. We were dressed carefully and standing straight. We had combed our hair again before leaving the car.

Marshall seemed unhappy about something himself. He was cracking the knuckles of his thumbs over and over, their pop like the snapping of wishbones. He waved his hand at Happy Sam's warbonnet.

"You don't have to wear that," he said.

"You pay the full price, you get the full treatment," Happy Sam told him. He fingered the folded bills already tucked in his breast pocket.

"Where'd you get that anyway?" Marshall asked him.

"Satisfied customers," Happy Sam answered. "Satisfied customers. But you know, you don't have to worry," he told Marshall, opening a ragged pamphlet to the words he used to bind couples together. "I have respect." Happy Sam snapped his fingers at his sons, who launched into a bouncy song, something like a polka.

I want to remember the words Marshall and I gave one another, the promises we spoke into the wind, standing on a South Dakota plain. But I don't remember the vows. I don't remember saying my name, Maxine Bullhead.

Instead I see the limp turkey resting on a bench, its broken neck dangling over the side, beak dipped toward the ground. I see Happy Sam's sons in the background, their instruments slack in their hands, mouths open, eyes fixed on the grass. I see Happy Sam sweating in his suit, wetting the feathers of the warbonnet that framed his face. And I remember feeling the sudden weight of sin—tired, well-handled sin passed from hand to hand—slam against my heart.

"You're married," Happy Sam told us as I struggled to catch my breath. "It's over," he said when I didn't move. Happy Sam pulled off the warbonnet and wiped his dripping forehead on the arm of his suit jacket. He slung the warbonnet over his shoulder and walked his boys into the house.

Marshall took my hands and squeezed them too hard. "Let's get out of here," he whispered. And we did.

⌒ ⌒

It was five years later that Herod Small War caught me after church. "You visit the doctor," he counseled, grinning mischievously.

I tried not to hope too hard. I tried not to let my dreams run loose. But Herod was right. Marshall and I were finally going to have a child. Between us we knew he would be a boy named Jasper. We knew what he would look like. In bed together at night we drew pictures in the air. Jasper would be a singer, his voice would cry and sing, bringing back the old days. Jasper would be eloquent like the ancestors. We would close our eyes to hear him speak. Jasper would expand our married circle, increasing the love between us. Jasper would forever seal the busy mouths of rumor weavers who strung their looms each morning with deft tongues, claiming our childlessness was proof of what marrying a Bullhead would do.

Marshall worked hard at whatever jobs he could get. He helped local farmers with harvesting and rode with ranchers to tend cattle. He threshed, branded, and butchered. He dreamed as hard as I did.

On my last visit to the Indian Health Clinic before the delivery, the doctor called the two of us into his office. He was a new doctor from somewhere in the East where people spoke too quickly. His glasses kept slipping down his nose. He looked frightened. The three of us sat in silence for long moments. Marshall shifted. We were both too large for the small, hard chairs.

Suddenly the doctor was telling us, "The baby is

already dead. It happens sometimes. We can't find a heartbeat."

I wanted to offer my own. *Give Jasper mine,* I thought. *Give him something of mine to warm his blood.* The doctor's voice was pitched too high, on the verge of hysteria. I wondered why this doctor was so upset for us.

Marshall had risen. He was arguing with the doctor. I wanted to rise too, but Jasper weighed me down like an anchor. Marshall told the doctor his science wasn't the last word—it was only good up to a point. Marshall looked stronger than I'd ever seen him. He looked like he could hammer the doctor into the ground with just a few more sentences.

That's why he's upset, I realized. *He's afraid of us.* Who knows what a wild Indian will do to a white doctor from the East. Too much John Wayne. Too many Hollywood hatchets dripping stage blood. I calmly watched the doctor in his terror, purposely concentrating on him to keep my mind from slipping off sideways, running out of the clinic and scrabbling on all fours to the top of Angry Butte, where its last trace of understanding would explode into slivers of howling sound.

～ ～

The baby was due that week, so the doctor told me he wouldn't induce labor for two days. It was still possible to deliver naturally and avoid an operation. Marshall was convinced there was hope. He worked harder than ever.

When I was alone I kept my eyes busy, off the rounded hill of my stomach rising like a burial mound of hidden dead. I had my mother make special moccasins for Jasper, just in case. But I wouldn't allow them in the house. The ancestors might become anxious to fit them on his feet.

Marshall took me to the Indian Health Hospital when I went into labor. The pain made me happy. The pain stretched a smile across my face. Marshall shivered in the car. His hands drifted over the steering wheel, locking and unlocking. Slim twists of prayer tobacco were spread on the dashboard, their spicy smell sweetening the air. Marshall was watching the straight, empty road.

"Don't give up," he told me. They could have been my son's words.

"No," I told my husband, "we won't." Pain was my son's voice. He was trying to be heard. I listened and listened. My body strained to hear until the whole world became the angry voice of pain and the scent of tobacco.

When we arrived at the hospital Marshall stayed with me until I was taken away to a yellow room.

"He's run off," I heard one of the nurses tell the doctor. She smiled at me and her features pinched together. "We'll get this over with as soon as possible," she said.

No. Don't give up. Voices were filling my head. My brain was swollen and tight with voices until I felt them exploding from my body: rushing from my ears, singing from my mouth, falling from my eyes, rising from my pores.

"Poor soul," the nurse was whispering, "he's probably off getting drunk and left her with this tragedy." She placed her hands on my knees and I felt the voices stab her flesh and soar to the ceiling.

"I see it time and time again," the doctor said. He didn't touch me. He was looking at his clean white hands as the voices slipped inside his jacket to lick his skin.

"It was a mistake to repeal," the nurse said. I knew what she meant. The Indian Liquor Law, prohibiting Indians from buying liquor, had been repealed only two years earlier. She was flushed and smug. She didn't notice that the voices had tipped her cap and were chewing on the nipples of her breasts.

"You're almost there," the doctor told me, "it'll be over soon."

No. Don't give up. The voices punctured his eyes.

Eventually the pain became quiet and the voices died. They scattered like petals, and the doctor and nurse crushed them underfoot. My son, Jasper, was silent in the nurse's arms.

"I want him," I told her. She shook her head, no, and moved toward the door.

I sat up and touched my feet to the cold floor. "You bring him to me right now," I told her, starting to rise.

"You'd better let her," the doctor said as he left the room.

I held my son, Jasper, in my arms. His body was light as a rag doll's, but his head was heavy. His thoughts must have petrified, layer upon layer. He was beautiful, like my mother. His lashes were very long, brushing down the rim of his cheeks. His body was perfect. It was hard to believe anything was wrong.

"Abu," I whispered. Sleep. *"Abu."* In the few minutes the nurse left me I let go of Jasper's spirit. I put my lips to the unfused well of his soft spot, whispering, *"abu,"* until it became a mother's song, and rocked him away.

When he returned later that same day, Marshall's hair was wet, making it spike and separate like quills on a porcupine. His face was dirty, oiled with dust, sweat, and tears. He took my face in his hands. They smelled of tobacco and were hot, as if he had just snatched them from a fire. When my tears hit his hand I expected a spitting hiss.

"It didn't work," he whispered, looking not at me but at a corner of the room where two yellow walls met in a gray shadow. "We prayed. We called on everyone we could remember, and see what happened." He was talking to himself, I thought. "See what happened," he insisted.

Marshall had driven to Herod Small War's place to

pray for Jasper. Their voices had joined me from across thirty miles and held me up when I brought death into the world. The ancestors they called on for help were sleeping. The ancestors were peeking at us from behind their hands but wouldn't look and wouldn't answer.

"It's because I'm a Bullhead," I told my husband, and I moved my eyes to the same spot in the corner of the room he had watched so carefully. I thought the gray shadow moved. I thought it quivered before settling back against the yellow walls.

I had felt empty after the delivery, light and hollow, ready to float up to the ceiling except for my heavy tears. But now I felt the familiar weight of old sin. Marshall had brought it back. He had seen its shadow in the corner. Its poison was released through my body, filling up the emptiness from my toes to the cracked-bone splinters of my mind.

"I'm a Bullhead," I repeated, and Marshall nodded. He took back his hands and stuck them in his pockets. His skin had cooled and dried, and my tears had ended. The only trace of them was a fine salt dust on my face and his fingers.

~ ~

Two months after Jasper was buried, brochures arrived from the Bureau of Indian Affairs. They were neatly folded, printed on slick white paper, proclaiming, CHICAGO—THE CITY BEAUTIFUL!

The photographs of Chicago caught my eye. They pictured elegant homes with broad staircases, grand pianos in apartments, flowers on every table; sailboats drifted on Lake Michigan, skirting the skyline; well-dressed Chicagoans smiled a welcome. I collected brochures from neighbors who were settled. I liked to stand them in a semicircle on the kitchen table so that when I rested my chin on its surface the brochures rose above my head like the city itself. I surrounded myself with Chicago's promises.

"I want to go to Chicago," I told Marshall one morning. He was eating oatmeal at the kitchen table, his bowl thrust into the center of my paper city. Marshall pushed the bowl away from him, nearly destroying the delicate lakeshore I'd created.

"So, you've got Relocation fever." It wasn't a question. He had seen the paper city rise.

"I want to get out of here," I nearly cried. Marshall's silence reminded me of my father's. I wanted to fill it up with all my reasons, but I didn't, because the truest reason of all was too large for my mouth. I couldn't tell Marshall that I believed Chicago would wash me in a clean light. Chicago would never know I was a Bullhead. The ancestors and *heyoka* spirits with their long memories would never see me in Chicago. I would walk barefoot on Oak Street Beach as Maxine Azure, and the sun would be so bright on my head I wouldn't have a shadow to fall forward or behind.

"Don't you know it's just another one of their tricks?" Marshall scolded me. He took down the brochures, placing them in a neat pile. His hands played with the corners. "They figure if they move us into the cities they'll get the last bit of land."

I believed him, and I didn't care. If the government was putting one over on me, I was putting one over on the higher powers. I was young enough to turn into Maxine Azure and have children we would raise in the city.

Marshall started to reach for me, his right hand moved to cover my own. But instead it jerked back to the brochures, tapping their edges on the table to even them up. His incomplete gesture made me cold the way I'd been cold every night since Jasper was buried. Marshall and I no longer fit together at night like a married puzzle but kept to our own sides, chilled separately by the moon. Sometimes his hand reached out to rub my back, but the hand was always cold and stiff.

Marshall was watching me. He'd never stared at me like that before because we were raised to understand it was rude. I could tell he pitied me. His eyes were sad and careful.

"Whatever you want to do, Maxine, that's what we'll do." I knew he would take me to Chicago because he felt sorry for me, something I would have hated a few months earlier. But now I just wanted to get away. I imagined in Chicago I would become the real Maxine, and my husband's pity would be transformed into wild admiration.

So we moved. Our house was government property to be turned over to another Sioux family, and our relatives took the furniture. Sitting Bull had been reburied in Mobridge, South Dakota, by white businessmen hoping to attract tourist dollars, but I went to his old grave anyway to walk the sacred ground. I visited Jasper before we left, smothering him with sage and wildflowers. "You'll always be my first child," I promised him.

When Marshall and I drove away from Fort Yates, North Dakota, I felt the road was lined with eyes. It wasn't until we'd left the reservation and hit the highway that we drove unseen. I wondered if that was what I had wanted all my life: to be invisible so that the sin lodged inside me would wink out, drained of all its terrible power.

～ ～

In Chicago, Marshall and I pretended we were new. We went to the Field Museum and Marshall Field's Department store. We stood beside the stone water tower. We had conversations about city life—the noise and traffic, all the different tribes we met at the Chicago Indian Center. We pretended to be angry at the BIA for fooling us, sending us pictures of the North Shore, where the wealthy lived, while we were caught in slum areas, chased from room to room by tenant cockroaches.

Mostly we worked hard. There was a lot of competition for jobs. I finally landed a waitressing job at an all-night cafe under the elevated train. All week I worked the late shift, coming home after eleven o'clock. Sometimes strange men walked closely behind me, so I took to strapping a thin knife to my forearm, just inside my sleeve. Marshall got home even later. He was the night watchman for the Indian Center. I liked having a key to the center, pretending the building was mine to be divided into large apartments for all the Indian people living in Chicago. Before I found my own job I would bring Marshall a late supper, and we'd sit for hours listening to the radio. Once I started work, I missed this chance for us to be together because we slept most of the day, and when we weren't sleeping the bright light made us shy, highlighting the fact that very little had actually changed.

Marshall's increasing silence was too much like my father's. It had a power I couldn't ignore. It could fill a room, doubling on itself, leaping from floor to wall to ceiling like a runaway flame, or it could drain the room like a sump pump, sucking at the bottom of my shoes.

I became homesick and wrote more often to my mother. One evening on my way to work I stopped by the post office just before closing to pick up a package. My mother had sent us *wasna*—a Sioux delicacy. She had packed the small round balls, consisting of ground chokecherries and corn meal, in wax paper inside a coffee can. On impulse I decided to call in sick to work and share the *wasna* with my husband.

I enjoyed the cold walk back to the Indian Center. I had never seen so many trees together as in the city, and I liked to walk on the bright leaves collecting on the ground.

I unlocked the heavy front door of the Indian Center, shutting it behind me with my hip and shoulder. The coffee can was cold from the walk and my cheeks were numb. I had no idea where Marshall would be, the building covered half a city block and was five stories high. I started down in the basement, slowly making my way to the fifth floor. Of course he was in the last place I looked, the chapel on the top floor. An Indian minister held services there every Sunday, which I liked to attend because his sermons were always on the edge of losing control. I imagined it had something to do with the setting: bloodred velvet drapes dropped from ceiling to floor, covering the four walls. The air was thick and oppressive. I had the feeling I was inside a human heart.

This time when I entered the chapel I noticed a drape had fallen from the wall. I heard voices. I don't remember walking toward the voices but I must have, because suddenly my feet trampled red velvet. Somehow the coffee can had fallen and the plastic lid popped off. Precious *wasna* rolled across the carpet. I found my husband wrapped in red velvet like a king, a woman curled to him. Marshall jumped away from her when he saw me. He wasn't careful and his movements exposed her body. Her face made no impression—it was very white and the features seemed smudged. Her black hair was thin and stringy. But her body offended me. Stretch marks on her breasts and belly marked her fertile; she had children. Her nipples were the pressed shape of a nursing mother; they had lived.

Marshall stood before me in his shorts. I realized I was still his height.

"What're you doing here?" he asked me. He looked desperate. He couldn't look me in the eyes so he discovered the *wasna*. "*Wasna*," he whispered stupidly.

I had choices then. I felt one in each hand. It was the sin that decided me—my great-grandfather's original sin swelling to fill me, pushing my organs aside, displacing my heart. I became the sin that was inside me from the time of my birth, and wrestled my husband to the ground.

I pinned his legs between my own and he twisted, slippery with sweat. The chapel was silent but for our breath like two snakes spitting fear. Our hands were clasped, finally warm again as they had been when we made Jasper. We wrenched arms, rolling over and over the *wasna* until it crumbled, dusting our bodies. I pushed Marshall's face into the red velvet, my knee on his neck, but he reared and threw me off. Now he was on top, his body crushing me. For a confused moment I wondered if we would make love.

The sin saved me. It was speaking aloud, its voice echoing in the chapel. *The blade. The blade.*

Marshall was sitting on my rib cage and my arms were raised above my head.

He has no respect. He thinks you killed Jasper. The sin spoke Sioux now. *The blade.*

Marshall had relaxed for a moment. We were both tired but I was fueled by sin. In that instant I reached inside my sleeve and pulled out the knife, slim and light as a razor. I stabbed Marshall in the heart. It was a completed act.

I held Marshall in my arms as he died, and our last words were all in Dakota so the shaking white woman wouldn't understand.

"I'm sorry," he told me, his pierced breath breaking the words apart. "We should never have left."

I shook my head. It wasn't Chicago or Relocation. But I could only whisper, "I love you," and cover his body with mine to keep him warm.

When the police came I said good-bye to my husband, and I could walk in a straight line. I knew who I was. I knew as I sat in the squad car, watching the dark streets of Chicago. I was Maxine Bullhead.

⌐ ⌐

I am beading moccasins for my husband, Marshall

Azure. I am beading the soles so I will see his flashing footprints in the sky.

Marshall is teaching Jasper to dance the old way. I can see them moving together when I close my eyes. Lieutenant Bullhead is dancing with an eagle feather fan. His body shakes with joy when he bends at the waist. Sitting Bull is singing the song. His voice is high. He is smiling because they are all together.

I cry over my beadwork and prick my fingers. It is hard for me to sit up straight on the edge of my cot because sins weigh me down, heavy as cannonballs welded to my shoulders.

Sins are at the center of my headache, slicing my thoughts into wedges. The sins are a pounding fluid, ripping through my arteries with a hot fire like gunshot in the bloodstream.

First Fruits

John Harvard, who as it turns out is not *really* John Harvard, contemplates his bronze-tasseled shoes and will not look me in the eye. He sits comfortably atop his pedestal, limbs remarkably relaxed for a statue. His left hand rests easily on the arm of his straight-backed chair, but there is something about its position that makes me think at any moment he may reach down to adjust his knickers. No, he remains static, for we have caught him between breaths of his great iron lungs.

I glance sideways at my father—the musician, Melvin Shoestring—and wonder if he knows how like him I am becoming. I have imagined this statue alive, just as I know my father has.

"This sculpture is popularly known as the statue of three lies," says Jean, our Harvard Student Agencies tour guide. I admired her from the first, for she is still in school but already a professional. Her crimson blazer and gray pleated skirt are perfectly pressed, her golden hair is French-braided in one neat plait, and her complexion is flawless.

"Three lies." My father echoes Jean.

"Lie number one," she continues. "It isn't clear *who* the actual model for this statue was, since no likeness of John Harvard exists. Lies two and three: you'll notice at the base here it states that this college was founded by John Harvard in 1638. In fact, it was founded by a legislative body two years earlier. It was named after Harvard out of gratitude, since he bequeathed the college eight hundred pounds and his extensive library."

I cannot actually see the words Jean is pointing to, for a dozen other people, including my father, have pushed eagerly forward to get a better view. Some of them look ready to climb into Harvard's lap. One elderly gentleman who leans on his umbrella as if it were a cane, elbows his wife, whispering, "It's Harvard. You'd think they'd get their facts straight."

She hushes him as if he has spoken aloud in church.

My father emerges from the huddle of tourists. "Did you see it?" he asks, pointing at the statue with his lips, a gesture I have seen made only by Indians. I nod my head, because otherwise he will clear a path for me and trace the words with his finger as if I am still five years old and learning to read by sounding out the letters, one at a time.

Jean surges forward, moving purposefully down one of the narrow paths that crisscross Harvard Yard in a complicated design, like strings in a game of cat's cradle. My father is right behind her, millimeters away from stepping on the backs of her heels. He doesn't watch where he is going; he's consulting the book he brought on this tour, his fingers like thick cigars thrust between its pages to mark pertinent passages. It is Alden T. Vaughan's historical work titled *New England Frontier: Puritans and Indians 1620–1675*. My father winks at me and shakes the book. We must be approaching the site he has been so anxious to see.

I am a little behind and to the right of him, at the edge of the flock. I want to see him as a stranger would, sketch him carefully in my mind because he will be leaving soon, for the first time in all my seventeen years. My father is the darkest member of this group, his skin like stained walnut beside Jean, who is pale as silver birch. He wears his black hair in two braids, but he and I are the only ones who know how short and sparse they are. He has wrapped them in otter skins, which trail to his thighs and kick out with each step he takes. They are not so much tradition as vanity, these hair ties and his cowboy boots with two-inch heels. My father is full-blooded Sioux, or Dakota as we call ourselves, but he is short for one of our tribe, a good half-head shorter than me. I take after my mother, who was six feet tall. For the first time, I notice that my father's jeans are too tight. But I don't think it's an attempt to appear sexy so much as a refusal to acknowledge that he has put on weight. I look into his face, which is strong, balanced, and smooth. It could have been hewn from one unblemished trunk of wood. His eyes glimmer with some mischief, and I almost pity Jean. My father will not be silent much longer.

After Jean has shown us Matthews Hall, my father speaks up. "What do you know about the Indian College?" he asks.

"Excuse me?" A wisp of hair has escaped from Jean's braid, and she carefully tucks it behind her ear.

"We're near the site of the Indian College," my father continues. "It was located behind this building." He cracks open Vaughan's volume and holds it out as proof.

"Really? I've never heard of it." Jean isn't ruffled in the slightest. "Why don't you tell us about it," she says.

Good for you, Jean, I am thinking. *You handled him just right.*

My father leads us to the back of Matthews Hall and spreads his arms. "This is about where it was. The Indian College, completed in 1655. It was the first brick building in Harvard Yard, two stories tall, and meant to house Indian students."

I have to give my father credit; the group looks interested.

"The Puritans—and you better believe they haven't been the only ones—felt that if you educated Indians, you could convert their souls." My father stares at me for a long moment before continuing. "Harvard was founded in part to help accomplish that goal. Here, let me read you this." He smiles, and balances the history book in his palm the way a minister wields his Bible.

"'President Henry Dunster took seriously the statement in Harvard's charter of 1650 that the purpose of the institution was *the education of the English and Indian Youth of this Country.* Dunster hoped *to make Harvard the Indian Oxford as well as the New-English Cambridge.*'"

Jean has removed a small notebook from her blazer pocket and is taking notes. She and the others wait expectantly.

"We were even a fund-raiser selling point," Dad tells them. "In 1643 a pamphlet called *New England's First Fruits* was printed to promote Harvard's cause. The first item on there was about the conversion and preparation of Indians."

"Did any graduate back then?" Jean asks.

"Just one, though several attended for a time, and they all came to sad ends, too. Caleb Cheeshateaumuck, a Wampanoag from Martha's Vineyard, graduated in 1665. His native language was Algonquin, but he mastered Latin, Greek, Hebrew, and, of course, English. He died a year after graduating, of consumption."

There is a soft murmur of sympathy in the group, and the gentleman with the umbrella shakes his head.

Jean is a trooper. "I thank you," she tells my father. "This has certainly enlightened us all."

She is not in the least sarcastic, and her gracious behavior catches my father a little off guard. He is so used to people who want to shut him down before he gets started, who want the past to remain there. I take the book from him and sling my arm around his shoulder, because this minor triumph has left him looking oddly defeated.

~ ~

The tour has ended, and my father and I stroll through Harvard Yard, where I will be living for the next year.

"What do you think, George? Will it suit you?" Melvin Shoestring, itinerant musician and sometime scholar, stops to face me. His hands weigh heavily on my shoulders.

"I belong here," I tell him as confidently as I can. I don't want him to leave feeling uneasy. I place my own hands on his shoulders and we are locked together, father and daughter. He nods his head sharply, satisfied.

"You'll be okay," he says to himself.

I think I am here because I sound exotic on paper. Even my name, Georgiana Lorraine Shoestring, makes me somewhat memorable. I have no transcripts to speak of since my father and I travel each year from Seattle, Washington, to Sarasota, Florida, and places in-between.

Unless my father is doing research for a new album, in which case we hole up in Chicago so he can study at The Newberry Library. He is a thoughtful, academic composer when it comes to his lyrics. The music is already on tape by the time he gets to the words, his steel guitar plucking the melody, tearing it out of his head. He chooses a different moment in Indian history for each album, his most recent being *First Fruits,* a collection of songs describing Puritan and Indian encounters in the seventeenth century.

Without meaning to, Dad put the idea of Harvard in my head. Until his talk of the college's history I hadn't made any future plans, content to read my books, help my father set up his sound equipment, and watch him perform from the rear of dark smoky rooms. I was intrigued to hear of an institution steeped in tradition. I thought it must be a place of stories, and I wanted to discover them. Unaware of the odds against my acceptance, I decided to apply.

I am self-educated, which means I have read everything I could lay hands on. The trunk of our taped-together midnight blue Buick is always full of used paperbacks and marked-up textbooks I have consumed like a locust. I was fearful of the college entrance exams, which even a heathen such as myself must endure, but I found them manageable and did quite well. After all, I had several discarded study guides to help prepare me.

Ironically, I don't think any other college would have accepted me; certainly we didn't have money for more than one application, and my father doesn't believe in fee waivers. I think Harvard admires the pathologically curious, the eccentric, unfettered mind enough to sometimes forego the formalities. So here I am in Cambridge, Massachusetts, towering above my father yet ready to curl within the cave of his chest. We have already smoked out my dormitory suite with prayer tobacco to banish whatever evil may linger there. My roommate hasn't arrived yet, which, I'm ashamed to say, is a bit of a relief.

My father and I are standing beside the wrought-iron bars of Johnston Gate. He is preparing to leave. The setting sun has striped the sky behind his head, and the blazing design of red to purple reminds me of a Pendleton blanket. What will he say? What should I tell him? We are Dakota and so are uncomfortable with physical affection. My father does what is most important. He takes my right hand between his callused palms and pumps it vigorously. He squeezes my hand and looks into my eyes.

"Don't you forget," he whispers.

I am slow to return to my room in Lionel Hall. I kick a square stone along the path, enjoying the skittering sound it makes. Harvard Yard is nearly deserted. I suppose my classmates are busy getting to know their roommates. As I approach Lionel, something stops me, a thickening of the atmosphere. I smell the tobacco my father and I burned in the small rooms. There is a taste in my mouth—something too sweet, like an overripe nectarine. There isn't much light in this part of the Yard. I am surrounded by dim shapes and shadows, but I can smell the grass and the trim hedges of arrowwood, and even the tangled ivy stitched to the brick facades of our dormitories. This place is abruptly alive.

I can't help but think that my father's presence—his prayers made of smoke sent directly to the eagles—has not expelled evil so much as invited a variety of spirits. The ones he taught me to recognize. From all my reading I know I am not supposed to believe in these specters, but I do. In our travels my father has pointed them out to me: shambling along the side of the road in a heavy coat, balancing on the rim of a rooftop like a tightrope performer, huddled behind the chair in a hotel room, or even hopping across the hood of our moving car, agile as a greyhound. Perhaps my father has turned Harvard Yard inside out, shaken its contents loose. I feel, rather than see, clouds collecting above this plot of land enclosed by a tall iron fence. Forces are gathering, whether they be atmospheric or spectral. I cannot ignore them. I believe and disbelieve in them because I am

Dakota, and to remain Indian in this world one must learn to accommodate contradictions.

～ ～

I have just emerged from the shower, swathed in towels, when I stumble upon my roommate. She stands in the living room surrounded by a matched set of luggage. She is alone, and I notice that her hands are shaking as she tries to light a cigarette. When she sees me, she drops it on her desk and climbs free of the piled suitcases.

"You're handsome," she says. She hugs me fiercely. My arms are pinned to my damp sides, but I wouldn't know what to do with them anyway. I'm not used to this sort of thing. She pulls back and thrusts out her hand. "Good to know you," she says as our hands move up and down. And there is something about the way her strange indigo eyes whisk across my face that makes me think she *does* know me. She has discovered me at a glance.

Her name is Allegra Kushner-Wallace, and she is alone because her parents are embroiled in a three-day argument they were anxious to resume after dropping her off.

"What about?" I ask.

"Well, surface level is whether they should get a summer place in the Adirondacks. Honesty level is why my Dad can't stand being around my mother. Frankly, I could use a vacation from both of them."

Allegra realizes what she has said, and in a moment we are both hysterical, laughing until we are unable to breathe and must make our way—arm-in-arm and bent over double—to the narrow bunk bed.

"Just a four-year vacation," she says, and we are howling, hiccoughing. Allegra has curled herself into a ball, tight as a possum, her little feet kicking helplessly as tears leak onto my comforter. It is a relief to laugh this hard, until our muscles ache and we are drained of nerves, farewells, insecurities.

As we unpack our bags and straighten the small suite of rooms—bedroom, living room, and bathroom— I watch Allegra as closely as possible without actually staring. I've never really had a non-Indian friend, since my father and I hit mostly reservations and urban Indian enclaves in our travels. I imagine that I know *something* of mainstream society. I have read so much about it, and studied the classics written by authors my father has dubbed The Great White Men and The Peculiar White Women.

Allegra will be my introduction to this new world, although she doesn't realize it. *I cannot presume to understand a culture on the basis of one person's behavior,* I tell myself. But I watch Allegra just the same. I observe that she wears wine-colored lipstick and heavy rice powder makeup. A branch of blue veins cuts beneath her paper white skin, all of them delicate but for the one pulsing across her forehead. She is shorter than I am but taller than my father, and her slight frame reminds me of the turquoise damselflies I have seen skimming elegantly above lake water.

We finish unpacking and tape the freshman orientation schedule on our bedroom door. Allegra perches on her desk, combing her auburn hair, which is short and fine on top, swinging like a full skirt when she turns her head.

"So tell me," she says, "what's the deal?"

I don't know what she means. She points her pink comb at me. "I mean the story. What's your story?"

~ ~

I dream about the mares' tails. I left them out of the story I told Allegra, skipped that part and moved on to the road adventures my father and I shared these past nine years. But the tails are there, twitching in my brain, reminding me—as if I need reminding—that they will always be part of the story. Upon waking I can still see them for just an instant, streaked across the ceiling, until darkness claims them.

I was eight years old, seated beside my father in the rocking car of a Ferris wheel, when I first saw the wispy formation of cirrus clouds he told me were mares' tails. He showed me how the sky was crowded with horses, packed together with their flanks to the oncoming storm, so all we could see were their silver tails streaming behind them in the wind. My father and I never missed a carnival if we could help it, although my mother didn't share this particular enthusiasm and waited for us at home.

We had a base of operations back then, on the Standing Rock Sioux Reservation in North Dakota: an old two-story farmhouse, stripped of its paint by the elements. Because my mother felt the ceilings were low, she moved uncomfortably through the rooms, hunched in the way of an older woman. She liked to sit on the back steps where she could admire her garden and stretch her limbs and her long spine.

The night of the mares' tails, my father and I stopped along the floodplain on our way home, to pick bluebells for my mother. They stretched across the flat field like drooping nuns settled in pews. As my father filled my arms with flowers, our house was burning. By the time we drove into our yard, a sudden rain, predicted by the clouds, had doused most of the flames. But the house was already a skeleton—an artifact we'd uncovered on the prairie.

No one ever learned what started the fire. The best guess was a problem with the ancient electrical wiring. Our own people believed it was *heyoka* spirits, who can be malignant in their mischief. For several months after the fire I could see them in my dreams: small as children and squatting in a circle beside our house. They rubbed their stiff little fingers together until sparks caught, glowing against their dark skin. They blew into cupped palms and their hands ignited, blazed vividly yet were not consumed, like the burning bush of Moses' vision. They patted the house then, stroked its splintered panels, traced the windowsills with their scorching fingers, each caress yielding a string of fire. And when my mother's spirit fled through the chimney, wafting above their upturned faces, they reached for her. One grabbed her by the hair but she pulled free, and he was left with a sable strand that quickly sizzled to ash.

~ ~

"Wait up! Hey, wait for me!" I slow down so Allegra can catch up to me. "You've *got* to learn to pace yourself," she says. She takes quick, shallow breaths, head averted so I will not hear her panting. Her royal blue running suit has been stained by perspiration; the pattern is a perfect V pointing from her collar to her chest, as neat as if it had been drawn.

Allegra is teaching me to jog and it is wearing her down. I am a difficult subject. I want to run flat out, my legs become pure speed until I feel the sharpness of the air, its planes and angles, cut into my flesh. I imagine that with enough velocity I will break through the barrier, shatter the air like a pane of glass or a bright mirror and emerge into light. A mystery. A new story. But Allegra's voice is like a hand on my arm, and it pulls me back. We are paused beside the Charles River, jogging in place so we don't cramp our muscles or shock our systems.

"You can go farther if you go slowly," Allegra lectures.

I feel my head moving up and down, cooperatively, but I know this is a fallacy. *If I am quick I can get to the other side,* is what I am thinking.

As we return to our room, Allegra scolds me like a mother. "You study the way you run, George. You're going to burn yourself out."

"But I want to *know,*" I tell her.

Allegra chuckles deep in her throat, a warm sound. "There's something you ought to realize, *mon amie,*" she says. "There isn't a soul alive who can know everything. Not a blessed soul." This last remark is spoken gravely, in the voice she uses to imitate her father.

"But a person can die trying," I answer, using that conjunction again—on the defensive. Allegra means well, she worries when she sees me attack a syllabus and tear through the reading assignments, getting far ahead of the schedule. I have never learned how to learn. I am not patient. I don't like my facts measured and tastefully arranged. I sit in class and take notes because it is expected, but I sometimes want to stand up and shout, "Yes, but what do you *believe?* What can you *see?*"

My father has always seen beyond the surface of things, what he calls the distracting reality. He has this telescopic, microscopic view—both large and small—peeling back layers and getting to the spirit of things. His presence has faded, however, just as the smoke of burnt sage dissipated, was replaced by Allegra's cigarette smoke and the fragrance of her cologne.

～ ～

As I head for class each morning, I find myself going out of my way, wandering behind Matthews Hall to that spot where the Indian College once stood. I must look like everyone else as I stand here, wearing jeans, a sweater, and a backpack over one shoulder, but I have uncommon expectations. I am looking for Caleb Cheeshateaumuck. If my father were here, we would have spotted him by now, perhaps seated high in the air toward the crown of the sycamore tree, or stretched on his side in the dense grass, his suit sparkling with dewdrops.

I am haunted by this young man who has been dead for over three hundred years, or, more accurately, I *wish* to be haunted by him. I have developed a plan to flush him out that consists of tempting him with a small package of Grandma's Old-Fashioned Molasses Cookies, which are a special favorite of my father's. I open the bag to release the spicy aroma and place it in a cradle of branches near the base of a thick bush.

"An offering," I say.

I was taught to believe that time is not a linear stream, but a hoop spinning forward like a wheel, where everything is connected and everything is eternal. In this cosmology, I am here because Caleb came before me, and he was here in anticipation of me. We are bonded together across time, and I will recognize him when I see him. Will he recognize me?

Allegra has made me over with the assistance of her friend, Adrienne, a fellow New Yorker who lives in the suite directly above ours. They cut my hair so that it is short in back and longer in front; the sides sweep below my cheeks like black wings. They have recommended bronze berry lip gloss for my mouth, and drawn pearl pink eyeshadow across my eyelids so that they look opalescent as abalone shells. Allegra even coated my eyelashes with Vaseline, using a tiny brush I find difficult to handle.

I take one last look before leaving for class.

"Kokepe sni ye," I tell the empty air. Don't be afraid. And then I whisper, "It's me, your Dakota friend," just in case Caleb Cheeshateaumuck has been fooled by Allegra's handiwork into thinking I am a *wasicun*—a white girl, leaving cookies for the squirrels.

⌒ ⌒

Allegra charges into our room, slamming the door shut behind her. I barely look up from my notebook. Allegra always bangs the door. She tosses her coat on the fossilized rocking chair we rescued from an alley Dumpster—it had looked alive to us, moved by the wind to rock unsteadily on the Dumpster's metal lid.

"There's something to this," she says, dragging her chair beside mine and folding into it, legs drawn up so her knees frame the point of her chin.

"Something to what?" I ask, but I already know and I don't want to hear it.

"This assignment. I keep seeing things that a few days ago would not have even registered. Things that would've seemed completely insignificant. But now I can't stop noticing them." Allegra's pale skin shimmers in our dim room, she seems lit from within, a sheath of parchment wrapping pure light.

"Like what?" *Stop asking questions,* I tell myself, but perhaps she can provide some insight, help me understand why I am blocked by this exercise.

"I was studying at Hilles," she tells me, just a notch above whispering. "I started looking all around me, and I noticed this girl sitting a few feet away. She'd taken off her shoes and she wasn't wearing any socks. She had friendship bracelets on both her ankles, and her ankles were crossed. They were so thin, just little white bones, like drumsticks laid down after a set. There was something exquisitely sad about them."

Allegra sighs and sweeps her hair forward, then

back. "I can't put my finger on what it means to me yet. But it means something. All these moments add up to *something*."

I can feel my head nodding. "Great material," I tell my roommate. I don't want her to see through me with those indigo eyes that look capable of perforating steel. I don't want her to know that I just don't get it.

Allegra and I share one class together: Expository Writing, which is mandatory for all freshmen. Our teacher, Stefan, is a graduate student who assured us on our first day of class that he has "happier things to do." We have written three papers for him so far, analyzing short stories and poems. After returning the last batch of papers to us, he sat quietly at the head of our long table, massaging his temples.

"These were more than adequate," he finally said, "but uninspired. You can all put together a perfectly competent composition—logical arguments, creditable technique. But where's the heart?" His palms slapped down on the table, and he lunged forward so suddenly a few students pulled back. He looked a little like a figurehead jutting from the prow of a ship.

"Where—is—the—fire?" With each syllable he smacked the table, and when he lifted his hands, the palms were red. "I want you to go forth and look at the world," he told us. "If you observe the usual closely enough, it begins to look *un*usual. Tell me what you see out there, don't worry about form. Keep a journal and describe what you have noticed."

Tomorrow we are expected to hand in the first part of our journals. I should be prepared. I have gone for long walks, gazing dutifully into passing faces, and stared at buildings until I could probably sketch them from memory. I have ridden the "T" into Boston and eavesdropped on the conversations of fellow passengers. I even wandered along the Charles River early one morning, watching members of the crew team knife through the mist in their sleek racing shells. I've written down my observations, described them in detail, but I haven't marveled at what I've seen. None of it strikes me as unusual.

What's wrong with me? I wonder, and then I notice I have written the question in my journal. I'm beginning to feel that the remarkable has been banished—at least temporarily—from my life. The things that have significance for me, an extraordinary weight, are those that are missing. Their absence is tangible.

My father has made off with the ghosts. I imagine them thronging behind his car, a great army of figures uniformly cast in sepia tones. And he has taken the stories with him too, even Harvard's stories. I can see them tied together like a bundle of pick-up-sticks, tossed in the Buick's cluttered glove compartment.

Allegra nudges me with her toe. "Hel-lo-o. Anybody home?"

Why does she see what she sees? I want to know. So I ask my roommate: "How do you think of yourself?"

"I have the body of a boy," she laments without pausing.

"No, I mean allegiance-wise, in terms of identity."

"Oh, that. I'm a New Yorker. An American. As far as religion goes, it's confused. I'm half Jewish and half Episcopalian. They cancel each other out so I guess you could say I believe in nothing."

Allegra pulls on her toes, then shoots one eyebrow high above the other, a trick I have seen her practice in the mirror. "What's this all about?" she asks.

"Just curious," I lie. She probabaly realizes it too, but it doesn't matter. Allegra's confidence has pumped into the air like steam. I know who I am as surely as Allegra does. If I cannot write with passion about the things I see, I will record what I don't see.

~ ~

In writing about him, I have uncovered Caleb Cheeshateaumuck's elusive spirit. It should have been plain to me earlier, where I would find him. For, of course, I will never catch him loitering behind Matthews Hall, tracing the outline of the Indian College's buried foundation with his restless strides. Caleb Cheeshateaumuck has reverted to the culture he was born into, embraced it fervently in death.

"I am Wampanoag," he tells me, and I can hear him

now that Allegra is sleeping and Harvard Yard is hushed.

He has returned to Martha's Vineyard, surrounded by thirty-seven gods who spin forth to greet him, animated as waterspouts. His relatives are all there, and his mother steps forward to help him remove the double-breasted woolen jacket buttoned to his throat. She has made him a full-length coat woven of turkey feathers. He slips it on and shrugs his shoulders.

"So light," he tells her.

His father hands him a gut-strung bow fashioned of witch hazel, and arrows tipped with eagle claws. Even his little sister offers a present: a basket of bright red pearplums, their flesh taut with ripe juice. Caleb strikes out on his own to reclaim the island, collecting small stones and the sun-dried corpses of sea horses and sand dollars. He scratches birchbark with his thumbnail, drawing geometrical designs he has learned studying Euclid's theorems. But the sap transforms the lines, rounds them out until they resemble etchings of bats and spiders.

Caleb Cheeshateaumuck finds the cove he has favored since childhood. A tangle of sea lavender flows from the grassy ledge above his head. He settles in the sand and sleeps. A painted turtle with slick red-and-green carapace pushes up from the sand to serve as a footrest. Starfish, swept in by the tide, ring Caleb's body like a constellation fallen from the sky. A spotted salmon leaps into his lap, offering itself.

I am ready to put down the journal and leave Caleb, when he opens his eyes and sits up. He shakes his head. I watch him comb through the pockets of his woolen knickers, finally brandishing a sheaf of pulpy yellow paper and a lead pencil he sharpens with a knife. He marks down letters, words, writing feverishly. I immediately grasp what he's doing: letting go of the languages. He folds the sheets into paper birds, and then launches them into the sea. One after the other they soar to life, sprouting lacy white feathers. They have become snowy egrets, and I watch them with Caleb as they land behind him in the salt marsh, where they wade gracefully through tall reeds. Caleb Cheeshateaumuck calls to them in what must be Algonquin—it is the only language he remembers.

My gift to him, across time, is a necklace of jingle shells. The delicate valves shimmer with an iridescent sheen and lay against his chest like a string of silver planets. Their music is the ring of wind chimes.

～ ～

Allegra and Adrienne are indulging in what they call "serious down time," taking a break from inorganic chemistry problem sets. They collect troll dolls with wild tufts of brightly colored hair and have spread them out on Allegra's desk. There are enough of them to constitute a small tribe. Adrienne is an expert with a needle and has created a wardrobe for the dolls: bib overalls, miniskirts, a tweed jacket, even striped pajamas. The two have separated the boys from the girls.

"How can you tell them apart?" I ask.

"Oh, it's easy," Adrienne says. "You can tell just by looking into their faces." Adrienne has small white hands and such sensitive skin she applies lotion three or four times a day. She has what she calls "titian" hair, cascading in waves down her back. My father would envy that hair.

"Well, George. Do you want to play?" Allegra asks me. "We're going to hold a mass wedding, like the Reverend Moon. Everyone gets hitched today."

"Go ahead and start," I tell them. "Call me when the real festivities begin."

I want to read Stefan's comments in my journal. I haven't had the nerve to check them before now. I felt sheepish and strange when I handed in the assignment, worried about what Stefan would think. Needlessly, as it turns out. Stefan used a red pen and has tracked the pages with tiny *Yes*'s, which gradually become larger and press into the paper more urgently. They seem to be moving toward a crescendo. On the last page he has written simply: *It lives*. He could be referring to the text, or to the spirit of Caleb Cheeshateaumuck, my compatriot. But I take it to mean my own soul, which was hidden for a time.

I hear the mailman in the entryway, and when he has gone I collect our mail. There is a postcard from my father. I immediately recognize the ostentatious, deeply chiseled features of the faces carved into Mount Rushmore. My father must be doing his tour of the South Dakota reservations. I know he didn't actually visit the Mount Rushmore Memorial. He hates it. "I'm not going to pay money to see the desecration of our place of worship," he said whenever we passed the Black Hills. His message comes to me when I most need it. He could have read my mind. Or maybe it was the hills, our hills rising against the sky like spiny steeples, murmuring sacred messages to my father, warning him that one was slipping away. He wrote a single sentence on the card, in his fat script: *Don't let them change you.*

I slip a powwow tape into my tape player, one of my favorite drum groups—the Wisconsin Dells Singers. When they come to the traditional swan dance, my feet tap restlessly against the floor.

Allegra and Adrienne have arranged the trolls in two neat columns where they pose, hand-to-hand, solemn pairs.

"You can turn that up," Allegra tells me. So I raise the volume until the air vibrates with drumbeats.

"What is that?" Adrienne asks. She is fluffing the chartreuse hair of her favorite doll.

"It's Winnebago music. This is what they call the swan dance."

"Have you ever seen it, you know, performed?" Allegra plucks the liner notes from the cassette case and squints at the tiny print.

"Sure. I've done it myself."

She cocks her head to one side, looking surprised. "Show me," she says.

"It's not the kind of dance you do alone," I explain. "Usually there's a line of young girls, moving around the drum like swans swimming in the water."

"Teach us then," says Adrienne.

Allegra nods her head. "I'm game."

We push back the chairs and kick a pile of newspapers under my desk. I move in front of them, executing the simple two-step. My arms are extended to my sides, rolling forward like oars dipping in water. They catch on quickly, Allegra behind me, and Adrienne behind her. We glide through the room, peeking back and forth to check our form.

"Again!" my friends cry out when we come to the end of the song. We reset the tape over and over.

A weight is lifting from my shoulders, dissolving in the air. I almost believe we could rise off the ground, propelled by the wings of our arms.

"I'll show you," I tell my friends. I shall carry them with me, coast above Harvard Yard high enough to see our shadows stretch across the buildings. I will their arms to follow mine, their every movement to match my own so that we can merge, the strings and needles flashing swiftly between us, stitching us together.

We have become one creature: a graceful, milk-pure swan with feathers soft as Chinese silk. We are a beautiful bird, lovely as the snowy egrets Caleb Cheeshateaumuck fashioned from pleated paper.

Indian Princess

It hurts me to see this young girl in a box, hands folded across the beaded handle of her eagle feather fan. It was only last week she used it at the powwow to cool herself down after a fast number. But now it is motionless, of no use to her, for she is dancing in that place where she will never tire, never stumble, never overstep the song by even half a beat. We dressed her in the fancy dance costume her mother, Crystal, completed just two weeks ago. The dress is red satin, cut to flare a little at the knees, which is the new style. Indian-head nickels cover the bust and arms of the dress, and it strikes me now that they are money rather than ornaments. It looks as though someone has scattered them across her chest, someone has sold her to the ground. Natalie stopped wearing the choker made of deer bones and brass beads with her costume, but Crystal has tied it around her daughter's throat to hide the ugly bruises. The Chicago Indian Center has consented to bury Natalie in the sash and beaded crown she won last week in the princess competition. The crown's cut beads sparkle so much it is almost shameful, cruel that anything she wears should be so alive.

But I am angry, too, and if I were alone I think I would scold Natalie, until I made her cry and sit up in this box to protest. It would surprise her, because I have always been so gentle, like an auntie to her, but I would not be gentle this time.

It was Harris who found you! I would say. I would point him out to her with my finger, perhaps call him over so she could look in his eyes and see that all the mischief has poured out. His eyes have changed color; they were a mild brown but have gone coal black as the pupils. They are depthless and cold.

You know he follows you everywhere, I would remind her. Harris is ten years old, and I can see that he will never be the same after finding his sister in the closet. He will never forget how her closet door scraped against the floor, the wood swollen and warped from the heat. He was holding the green iguana, bright as neon, which he's keeping for the summer as a favor to his teacher. He didn't say so, but I think he meant to scare Natalie, thrust the lizard in her face, but he found her hanging from a hook and didn't get the chance. She frightened him instead; she was so blue, so wrong-looking. He must have dropped the lizard, because we found it in the closet—Crystal and myself—when Harris dragged us by our flour-dusted hands into Natalie's bedroom, into Natalie's closet.

I know why she did this, and it is not a good reason. *It is not a good reason,* I would tell her, if Crystal were not around to overhear. *Natalie, you had a family, and you were smart, and you were beautiful,* I want to say. I would hold a mirror to her face and make her look. I could always tell she was Sioux, but now she looks like a full-blood, like her ancestors have truly taken her over. I touch the end of one thick black plait of hair, it has an edge almost like a blade, and I nod my head. There is no warmth or softness in this box.

Melvin King steps forward to pay his last respects, and I wonder if this pleases Natalie. *Is it enough? Is it what you wanted?* I feel like hollering. *Look at him. Is he such a prize?* For I know, even if Crystal does not, that Melvin King is the reason Natalie strangled herself with the belt of her costume.

He is eighteen years old and slouches against the box, not even carrying his own weight. I nudge him back. I am the guardian of this box. I make him stand on his own two feet and will not let him lean against Natalie for support. It isn't his fault, I know better than to blame him, but I cannot care for him since he *is* the walking Reason—ludicrous as it may seem. Yes, he can dance, I will admit, and I suppose his strong features are fine to look at. But they are the only strength in him.

He's been drinking, I want Natalie to know. He's swaying back and forth like a young tree in a windstorm, and I can smell it on him, too. I've heard that most nights he can be found at The Reservation—one of those Indian bars on Wilson Avenue. If he keeps drinking and fighting, he will lose the magic in his feet, lose that soft step, and his fine features will be swallowed up in the puffy face of an alcoholic. He's already lost one of his teeth, I notice, when he turns to me and opens his mouth in a terrible smile. It is meant to be polite, he is greeting an elder, but that smile falls on me heavier than the bricks of this building would if it suddenly collapsed. He shakes my hand and holds on to it.

"This is terrible," he breathes into my face. "How's Crystal doing?"

I make him take his hand back. "She's bad, but she's alive," is all I can say.

Are you alive? I want to ask him. I shouldn't be so hard; he doesn't know any better. His own mother was a heavy drinker who died of cirrhosis when he was three years old. He was with her, too, at the end. They found him curled beside her on the bed, attached to her breast as if he would never let go. He is pitiful, and I shouldn't resent him the way I do.

No one has said it to me, but I know there are two of them in this box: Natalie, and the seed planted by Melvin, who is a walking ghost.

Did you want to marry him? I ask Natalie silently, in my head, but it is not a question requiring an answer. I know. I can tell, even though Natalie isn't showing. I know she imagined she could change Melvin, turn him into a father who wouldn't drink, into a husband she could watch dance around the drum, his powerful legs lifting him off the ground, spinning him in his feather bustles until he resembled a bird.

You can't change other people, I should have told Natalie before now. But I was quiet because I thought she would figure it out for herself. I am seventy-two years old, and I lost my husband twenty years ago. I have learned so many things, but mostly this: no one can hold a person back from their mistakes.

It hurts me to look at this little girl who was here for just seventeen years—a blink of the eye—and to know that there is nothing I can do to raise her up and push her into Crystal's arms, and there is nothing I could have done to make her know that it was not a good reason. She would have looked at me the way children do when you tell them the truth. She was a good girl, so she wouldn't have rolled her eyes. But my words—my unwanted advice—would have spilled across her like a quick, gentle rain, not enough water to reach up and brush away.

How could she know that someday she wouldn't care for Melvin, wouldn't need him, or, if she still had feelings for him, they would have dimmed to become a safe sentiment? How could she predict that one day, if she lived long enough, small, small things would warm her and make her smile? I wish I could have made her understand that even a life such as mine can be deceptive. It is more than she thought it was, just as her own life was immeasurably precious.

She used to ride with me on the bus to the supermarket every week. By the time we were headed back home, my legs usually pained me, and the knee-high nylons I wore would be cutting into my flesh, so I would have her roll them down to my ankles. I taught her to position the shopping bags between her feet, making it hard for anyone to snatch them. I suppose she looked at me, sitting there with bunched-up nylons and bags pressed between my legs, and thought, *This sad old lady is not so smart. I hope I don't end up this way.*

I want to shake her, whisper in her ear: *I was happy on that bus. I watched you, and the people around me, and sorted through my memories. I was busy, while I sat there beside you, plumbing the mysteries of this life.*

Histories

Stone Women

My grandfather, Colvin Kelly, is hiding in a hole. His wife and eldest five children used spoons, tin cups, and copper pans to dig a hole near the stove in their two-bedroom cabin. It is lucky they have a dirt floor so my grandfather can crouch in a hole under the kitchen table.

My mother, Susan, and her sister Elsie find magazines for him to read in the shadows. Magazines are hard to find. I think the reservation priest lends them *National Geographic.* Susan and Elsie walk through town, looking for cigarette butts. Later, at home, they will make cigarettes for my grandfather to smoke under the kitchen table. My mother likes to watch the smoke rising mysteriously from the ground, winding between the ankles of seated children. Whenever a visitor stops by, the children warn their father, and he must pinch the end of his cigarette and close his magazine.

I imagine he shuts his eyes and listens to the houseguest. Will it be the police? Will they find him? Will they insult his wife and embarrass his children? It is

1935 and against the law for Indians to purchase or drink alcohol even though Prohibition has ended. The laws won't change for another twenty years.

My grandfather speaks old-time Dakota but looks more like a white man than any of his drinking buddies, so he can buy them all liquor once in a while. But someone has told on him, and the police are searching, waiting for him to surface, as they know he will when the urge to drink gets too strong.

I want to know what my grandfather is thinking. Does he speak English or Dakota in his mind? He rubs the stump of his left leg in the dark, the damp earth makes it ache more than usual. He must remember running away from Indian boarding school when he touches it. Perhaps he is just as frightened now as he was at age eleven, when his sweaty hands couldn't keep a firm grip on the boxcar ladder, and he fell beneath the train.

I want to sew him a Ghost Dance shirt. I want to use the softest buckskin and brightest paints. I will paint the history of our family on its front and back with such careful strokes everyone will say it is a miracle: Look, she has included our ancestors' vision of the coming intruder; she has included our move from the East to the West; there are the battles of White Stone Hill and Little Big Horn; there are our dead chiefs—Gall, Sitting Bull, Crazy Horse, Two Bears; there is the White Buffalo Calf Woman and her gift of the sacred pipe; there is Wounded Knee and the mass graves; there are our boys in World War I; there is her grandfather slipping under the train.

I will sew tassels of horsehair, and medicine wheels made of dyed porcupine quills on the shirt. I will trim its edges with long glass bugle beads so my grandfather sparkles in the sun. The Ghost Dance shirt will make him invisible to whites so he can move through this country like a man on a bold vision quest. The Ghost Dance shirt will heal his leg and cure his taste for liquor. He will be the tallest man in Fort Yates, North Dakota, on the Standing Rock Sioux Reservation. He will whisper my Dakota name, Wanakca Wastewin, the name of a rare prairie flower, as he walks along the Grand River, counting the water moccasins he sees resting on its shore, and he will smile, knowing that I am coming.

～ ～

My mother was born in 1925 on the Standing Rock Sioux Reservation, which extends into both North and South Dakota. Her parents were Yanktonnai Sioux (Dakota), and her great-grandfather was Chief Mahto Nunhpa (Two Bears), who led the Battle of White Stone Hill in 1863 and eventually became a Catholic convert.

"We should never have converted," my mother tells me, "that's the start of all our problems. We ticked off our ancestors by doing that, so now they won't help us."

But I imagine Two Bears must be doing his best,

helping me get good grades, moving my pen when it is heavy and the paper is silent, helping my husband when he operates on patients, helping my mother when she feels the pain of the world. Two Bears is trying to make amends for being taken in by that traveling priest, Father DeSmet.

~ ~

The log cabin where my mother lived as a child burned down long ago but she has taken me to its location. We can't walk near the foundation or scratch in the dirt of the old yard because it is ten feet underwater, flooded by the government's construction of the Oahe Dam.

"Goddamn that Oahe Dam!" my mother says. "This reservation was so little land to begin with, and now a good portion of it is underwater. Useless. That dam is greedy."

I dream that the Oahe Dam has a wide mouth and chunky teeth, its lips rasp like paper as it eats our reservation. I tell it to stop, stop, and it laughs, opening its mouth the way children do to be naughty. I see long grass and dirt lining its throat, and the bones of my ancestors caught in its teeth. The snap of its closing mouth wakes me up, and I realize the sound is my mother, unpinning her hair and dropping bobby pins into an old Vaseline jar.

~ ~

My mother takes me to see the Stone Woman and I am disappointed. Standing Rock is named after her; her figure rests on a brick pedestal outside the Indian Agency office in Fort Yates. She is so much smaller than I'd imagined.

My mother traces a finger over the rock to point out her features. "This is her face. You see how she's hiding it under her shawl? And this is the baby strapped to her back." I reach up my hand to pat the baby's back. My mother tells me the story of the Stone Woman as we stand beside her. I have heard the legend so often it can't be for my benefit. Perhaps my mother is scolding this ancestor-sister.

"Here she is, this pouting woman. You see how she is hunched and looking at the ground? They say she was always moody and a little spoiled. She was so beautiful, she was used to people admiring her and letting her get her own way.

"I believe she loved her husband as much as she could love anyone. But I don't think she was a very good wife. So her husband found a second wife with a sweeter disposition. He picked her out just before they took down the village to move to winter camp. This woman didn't move a finger to help. The second wife did all the work, took down the lodge poles herself and folded the skins. Everyone was set to go but this woman wouldn't budge. She sat on the ground, her shawl over her head, practically smothering the baby on her back. Her husband begged and threatened, tried everything to get her on her feet. But she pouted. She was good at that. They left her there, figuring she would follow eventually. The next day she still hadn't turned up so her husband and his brother went back to find her. They found her sure enough. Turned to stone, and the baby with her. That's what pouting will get you."

I rub the child's back a little more before leaving. The baby is the most tragic part of the story for me. I want to hold its heavy little body and hug it against me until it is warm.

～ ～

My mother was the third of eight children, four girls and four boys. She was closest to Elsie, who was a year older. People thought they looked like twins.

"I was always the responsible one," my mother complains, "even though Helen and Elsie were older. I made the boys mind and kept the place clean for Mama. I learned to cook as soon as I learned to walk."

Elsie was the mischief-maker and my mother was her timid accomplice. It was Elsie who wanted to know if she could still hear the tick of a buried clock. Elsie and her mother went to the Luger's store in town where Elsie swiped a clock.

"I'll put it back when I'm through," she reassured her sister.

They buried the clock behind their cabin in a hole only one or two feet deep.

"We could still hear that clock," my mother tells me. "The dirt didn't mess up the works. But it sounded more like a heartbeat than a clock."

My grandmother caught them and was furious, making them return the clock. But it is significant to me that my mother heard its heart beating in the ground. If there is magic, my mother will find it. If there are spirits, my mother will see them. My mother leaves the cleanest bones on her plate after a meal. The bones are usually cracked because she has eaten the marrow, which she says is so tasty. She tells me she cannot waste food because she was a dust bowl Depression child, but I am skeptical. When I see those little white bones I know it is just the fierce way my mother lives her life.

My mother is a genius; at least I have always thought it was quite clever of her to teach herself to read when she was three years old. The only book the family owned was on child labor, and my mother was desperate to learn the stories behind the sad faces in the photographs.

"It was the first time I felt close to white children. I looked at their faces and knew what they were thinking," she says. She read that book so many times she memorized it and can still quote passages and statistics in a rhythmic voice that fashions the text into a poem.

Sometimes she would sit by Sitting Bull's grave and recite for him. "We used to put his poor old ghost through hell," she tells me.

Sitting Bull was originally buried across the road from my mother's cabin. Later, white businessmen would dig him up and cart him away to Mobridge, South Dakota, hoping to attract tourist dollars. But when my mother was little, he was a benevolent presence. Children called on him to intercede with angry parents and prayed to him the way they prayed to saints when the nuns stood over them in church.

A few lonely tourists would straggle onto the reservation to visit his grave, and when they did, my mother and the other children would pretend they couldn't speak English so the tourists would take their pictures and talk about them openly. With smiling faces, Elsie and my mother would curse them in Dakota, using their hands to signal "drop dead" in Indian sign language.

"You were bad," I tell her.

"We were bad," she admits with a smile.

~ ~

I feel left out when my mother describes spectral visits.

"My father's mother came to say good-bye to me," she whispers, showing me a picture of a woman who looks like my mother in a long dress. "She died hundreds of miles away but her spirit came to me in the night. She watched me from the foot of the bed I shared with Helen, Elsie, and Theodora. You know Helen, she can sleep through anything. When she got up to go to the outhouse, she walked right through Grandma and didn't even notice. That's when I knew Grandma was dead."

"Weren't you scared?" I have asked her.

"No. She was always good to me. She had the sweetest smile. Why should I be afraid?"

I am afraid. I am afraid for her in the big bed, sleeping under the frost-lined ceiling. I am afraid the grandmother will reach for her and take her away somewhere she will have to stay, so she will never meet my father. I am afraid I won't be born. I am afraid my own dead grandmothers will look for me, lonely in the afterlife, which might be boring. They always liked to hear me sing and tell stories. I am also afraid they will never come. I will never see them again. They will never love me enough to push across the border that has separated us for so long.

So much fear, my mother would say. I think she would be disgusted. It is the white side coming out, she would accuse me if she knew. Only she would use the Dakota word, *wasicun,* to make me feel doubly ashamed. So I listen to her story and accept that she has no fear. I have enough for us both.

~ ~

My mother tells me about Indian boarding school. She covers her eyes with her hand.

Elsie and my mother were holding hands, attached to a line of Indian girls strung out across the hospital corridor. Sister Michael stood facing them, her round face pinched red by a wimple.

She has unhappy flesh, my mother was thinking.

The girls' faces were impassive except for Elsie's, her nostrils flared as they always did when she was annoyed. Sister Michael would probably beat her for it later, but she didn't care. Elsie was tough.

Sister Michael had brought them to the maternity ward so they would understand the consequences of sin. The girls heard women crying, sometimes screaming, which seemed to please their teacher.

"Listen carefully," she told them. "Listen, even if it is difficult. This is the pain Our Dear Lord visited on Eve for giving in to temptation. This is the curse that we carry throughout life as her descendants. This is the Lord's judgment."

"This is *chesli*," crap, Elsie whispered to my mother. My mother smiled and Sister Michael was quick to confront the sisters.

"You'll be the first in hell," she declared, pointing at Elsie. "But it will be hell on earth, too. You're heading right into the pain. You keep it up, keep being smart. You'll be sorry."

Sister Michael could have been reading Elsie's palm. My aunt's quick feet carried her straight to pain, which hounded her to the grave. Still a young woman, she was murdered by her white boyfriend in Rapid City, South Dakota. The local police didn't investigate because he was a prominent citizen and she was Indian. The reservation priest wouldn't bury her in the churchyard because of the wild life she'd led, so she was buried just outside the fence. I wonder if I would hear her ticking heart in the unconsecrated ground?

If there is any justice, Aunt Elsie is tap-dancing in the afterlife as she used to as a child. She was always Ginger Rogers and my mother was Ruby Keeler. She is chatting it up with her hero, Joe Louis, who is giving her boxing tips. She is sitting on her father's lap and they are reading glossy magazines together. She is designing her own angel's wings by plucking ripe feathers off unsuspecting saints. She is telling God off-color jokes, one after the other, until He coughs and wheezes.

If there is any justice, Sister Michael is pain's companion, and she is discovering that He is never satisfied. She is so tired and so depressed. She would like to walk away from Him, but every time she tries, He snatches her back with a hot paw.

My grandfather is hiding in a hole. His daughters pass food to him under the table. He has run out of cigarettes and read each magazine ten times from cover to cover.

He calls his favorite daughters. "Will you find me some cigarettes?" he asks them. He is talking to their bare feet. Before they leave he gives them a nickel he's been saving. "Enough for two ice creams," he says, reaching up to place the coin in Elsie's hand.

My mother notices that his extended hand is shaking, and the other is massaging his sore stump. She starts to cry.

"Don't be such a sap," Elsie hisses in her ear, dragging my mother into the sun. "You've got to be tough!"

On the way to town Elsie and my mother see Old Man Standing Soldier asleep on the bench in front of his cabin. "Beautiful dreamer," they croon together, watching him with quick, crow eyes. "Beautiful dreamer, wake unto MEE-E-E-E!!!"

Old Man Standing Soldier falls off the bench. "Get away from here!" he yells. *"Lila sica, lila sica,"* very bad, he scolds.

My mother laughs so hard she almost pees in her pants.

The sisters come across Mary Halsey in her white anklets and black patent leather shoes. Her parents work for the Bureau of Indian Affairs so they always have money, even in hard times. They make Mary take off her shoes and socks so they can try them on.

"You'll stretch them out. You'll get them dirty!" she wails.

"Don't be so stingy," Elsie says, pulling up the loose legs of her overalls to look at the pretty shoes on her feet. My mother thinks the shoes are too tight when it is her turn.

"Here," she says, and hands them back to the weeping Mary.

Elsie and my mother are looking for cigarette butts in the street. They place the treasured tobacco in their pockets and wipe their hands on their thighs. They want to put together a whole pack of cigarettes, beautiful, even, and sweet-smelling. They want their father to close his eyes as he smokes their cigarettes, blowing smoke rings that rise from the dirt floor to the ceiling.

Museum Indians

A snake coils in my mother's dresser drawer; it is thick and black, glossy as sequins. My mother cut her hair several years ago, before I was born, but she kept one heavy braid. It is the three-foot snake I lift from its nest and handle as if it were alive.

"Mom, why did you cut your hair?" I ask. I am a little girl lifting a sleek black river into the light that streams through the kitchen window. Mom turns to me.

"It gave me headaches. Now put that away and wash your hands for lunch."

"You won't cut *my* hair, will you?" I'm sure this is a whine.

"No, just a little trim now and then to even the ends."

I return the dark snake to its nest among my mother's slips, arranging it so that its thin tail hides beneath the wide mouth sheared by scissors. My mother keeps her promise and lets my hair grow long, but I am only half of her; my thin brown braids will reach the middle of my back, and in maturity will look like tiny garden snakes.

My mother tells me stories every day: while she

cleans, while she cooks, on our way to the library, standing in the checkout line at the supermarket. I like to
share her stories with other people, and chatter like a
monkey when I am able to command adult attention.

"She left the reservation when she was sixteen years
old," I tell my audience. Sixteen sounds very old to me,
but I always state the number because it seems integral
to my recitation. "She had never been on a train before,
or used a telephone. She left Standing Rock to take a
job in Chicago so she could help out the family during
the war. She was petrified of all the strange people and
new surroundings; she stayed in her seat all the way
from McLaughlin, South Dakota, to Chicago, Illinois,
and didn't move once."

I usually laugh after saying this, because I cannot
imagine my mother being afraid of anything. She is so
tall, a true Dakota woman; she rises against the sun like
a skyscraper, and when I draw her picture in my notebook, she takes up the entire page. She talks politics
and attends sit-ins, wrestles with the Chicago police
and says what's on her mind.

I am her small shadow and witness. I am the timid
daughter who can rage only on paper.

We don't have much money, but Mom takes me from
one end of the city to the other on foot, on buses. I will
grow up believing that Chicago belongs to me, because
it was given to me by my mother. Nearly every week we
tour the Historical Society, and Mom makes a point of

complaining about the statue that depicts an Indian man about to kill a white woman and her children: "This is the only monument to the history of Indians in this area that you have on exhibit. It's a shame because it is completely one-sided. Children who see this will think this is what Indians are all about."

My mother lectures the guides and their bosses, until eventually that statue disappears.

Some days we haunt the Art Institute, and my mother pauses before a Picasso.

"He did this during his blue period," she tells me.

I squint at the blue man holding a blue guitar. "Was he very sad?" I ask.

"Yes, I think he was." My mother takes my hand and looks away from the painting. I can see a story developing behind her eyes, and I tug on her arm to release the words. She will tell me why Picasso was blue, what his thoughts were as he painted this canvas. She relates anecdotes I will never find in books, never see footnoted in a biography of the master artist. I don't even bother to check these references because I like my mother's version best.

When Mom is down, we go to see the mummies at the Field Museum of Natural History. The Egyptian dead sleep in the basement, most of them still shrouded in their wrappings.

"These were people like us," my mother whispers.

She pulls me into her waist. "They had dreams and intrigues and problems with their teeth. They thought their one particular life was of the utmost significance. And now, just *look* at them." My mother never fails to brighten. "So what's the use of worrying too hard or too long? Might as well be cheerful."

Before we leave this place, we always visit my great-grandmother's buckskin dress. We mount the stairs and walk through the museum's main hall—past the dinosaur bones all strung together, and the stuffed elephants lifting their trunks in a mute trumpet.

The clothed figures are disconcerting because they have no heads. I think of them as dead Indians. We reach the traditional outfits of the Sioux in the Plains Indian section, and there is the dress, as magnificent as I remembered. The yoke is completely beaded—I know the garment must be heavy to wear. My great-grandmother used blue beads as a background for the geometrical design, and I point to the azure expanse.

"Was this her blue period?" I ask my mother. She hushes me unexpectedly, she will not play the game. I come to understand that this is a solemn call, and we stand before the glass case as we would before a grave.

"I don't know how this got out of the family," Mom murmurs. I feel helpless beside her, wishing I could reach through the glass to disrobe the headless mannequin. My mother belongs in a grand buckskin dress such as this, even though her hair is now too short to braid and has been trained to curl at the edges in a saucy flip.

We leave our fingerprints on the glass, two sets of hands at different heights pressing against the barrier. Mom is sad to leave.

"I hope she knows we visit her dress," my mother says.

There is a little buffalo across the hall, stuffed and staring. Mom doesn't always have the heart to greet him. Some days we slip out of the museum without finding his stall.

"You don't belong here," Mom tells him on those rare occasions when she feels she must pay her respects. "We honor you," she continues, "because you are a creature of great endurance and great generosity. You provided us with so many things that helped us to survive. It makes me angry to see you like this."

Few things can make my mother cry; the buffalo is one of them.

"I am just like you," she whispers. "I don't belong here either. We should be in the Dakotas, somewhere a little bit east of the Missouri River. This crazy city is not a fit home for buffalo or Dakotas."

I take my mother's hand to hold her in place. I am a city child, nervous around livestock and lonely on the plains. I am afraid of a sky without light pollution—I

never knew there could be so many stars. I lead my
mother from the museum so she will forget the sense
of loss. From the marble steps we can see Lake Shore
Drive spill ahead of us, and I sweep my arm to the side
as if I were responsible for this view. I introduce my
mother to the city she gave me. I call her home.

Reunion

Mama, I am eleven years old, sitting in an empty corner of the school library, playing God. I miss my father, as I know you do, and so I return him to us with a few careful scrawls of my felt-tip pen. I rush back in time, carry us, all three of us, to the year 1935. I am not yet born, I am not dreamed of, so I tread the air a little above your heads and breathe softly through my nose.

You are standing beside Sitting Bull's grave, no, you are leaning against the marker—a small tower of stones—with your arms crossed and your eyes hidden beneath black bangs. You are ten years old, barefoot, wearing coveralls of an unknown color, and what looks to be a halo behind your lowered head is actually a cloud of dust, blown there by the drought.

A car is coming, you can see it from at least a mile away. Sioux children leap onto the wide running board, and two lean dogs snap at the belching smoke this noisy car trails in its wake. I stir them with a finger, these characters, knock them all to either side because I want you to be alone with the man in the car. My father leaves the car parked in the road and walks straight to you. He doesn't know why. He doesn't know it is his unborn child telling him what to do.

My father is twenty years old and a Hamilton College man. His fraternity brothers must be looking for him right about now; they would never dream he is two thousand miles away, approaching an Indian grave in North Dakota.

You like to tease the white tourists by pretending you can't speak English. Sometimes they take your picture and offer you a nickel. You wonder what my father will do. He doesn't smile and he doesn't speak. He doesn't look the least bit warm in his heavy tweed jacket. He removes a pipe from an inside pocket and a leather pouch filled with fragrant tobacco. You have seen men smoke pipes before, but never one this small.

What can you possibly say to one another? I hold my breath and bite my tongue. I'm tempted to tease you young people, chuckle from the sky, saying, *Little girl, this is your husband. College man, this is your future wife. Twenty-five years from now you will give each other matching gold rings and you will promise to stay together and you will keep the promise until the day the college man dies.*

Finally I direct you both to speak. My father says, *Tell me about this beautiful country. I've never been here before.*

I make you speak English to my handsome father and I know you wish you could touch the thick brown waves of his hair. You tell him the stories you have already told me. You point in one direction and then in another. He gestures toward Proposal Hill with the gnawed stem of his pipe, and so you tell him other tales. You are bolder after so much talking and twice you have glanced quickly into his eyes. They are gray—silver storm clouds—and you laugh to yourself because your Dakota name is *Mahpiya Bogawin,* Gathering of Stormclouds Woman.

I whisper in your ear, *Yes, someday you will gather him in.*

Now it is my father's turn to speak and he describes his mother's home in Albany, New York. You cannot imagine his life, his summers at a lake cottage and his Greek and Latin, his football injury and his Phi Beta Kappa key. His family is "old," you come to understand. His ancestors traveled to the North American continent in the early 1600s. Years into your marriage you will say to his elderly mother, *Oh, your family is so old.*

And she will look up at you, up and up, because she is not quite five feet tall and you are a six-foot Dakota woman. *Yes, but yours is older,* she will tell you, firmly, graciously. As if you hadn't taught me that from the beginning.

My father is not a storyteller and hasn't much to say, but his reading voice could coax the stars from their bright positions, so I have him remove a slim volume of poetry from his jacket pocket. Emily Dickinson. You sit on the ground, your back pressed against Sitting Bull's marker, your knees drawn up to your chin. You trust this dapper young white man with a flair for the dramatic, I can tell. You scratch his name in the dirt with a thin crooked stick. You draw it with the right hand and he stands on your left, so he cannot see that you are adding your name to his.

I want to keep us all together at this grave site, young as we are. But I know if I do that you will never meet my father and marry and give me life. You will spend your days listening to poetry.

Have to go, my father says, slapping the dust from his tweed.

You remain on the ground, hugging your knees. You are already afraid of losing him. My father slips his hand in the pocket of his stylishly baggy trousers.

Here you are, he says cheerfully. He bounces a little on the balls of his toes.

I can see you are disappointed. What is it? A nickel, a dime, maybe a quarter. *Perhaps he isn't different after all? Perhaps he isn't special?* you're thinking.

But wait, I tell you. *Take a look.* My father has given you his Phi Beta Kappa key, and it glints from the small page of your palm.

This should belong to you. These are the last words you hear my father speak. He waves from the car window as he drives away. The Sioux children and their lean dogs are waiting for him at the bottom of the road. They'll chase him to the edge of the reservation.

You admire the key; you hold it up to the light as if

you could unlock the sun. You toss it and catch it, you press it to your lips, you squeeze it in the tight curl of your fist. You wonder why he's given you such a present, and I proceed to tell you, though you may not believe me. You say you aren't particularly smart, that you haven't done very much in life, but my father and I know that this is just another one of your stories.

You read so many books—you are my encyclopedia. You recite the history of my ancestors without pause, without forgetting a single detail—you are my memory. You speak up when others are afraid to—you are my voice. You notice what so many people would like to ignore—you are my vision. You imagine that I can do anything I decide upon—you are my dreams. You've shown me where the spirits hide—you are my imagination. You've challenged me to change my corner of the world—you are my conscience.

Mama, I am eleven years old, sitting in an empty corner of the school library, missing my father who has been gone for six months. I place the cap on my felt-tip pen because I no longer need to comfort and distract myself by playing God.

After school I tell you how I managed this first meeting in my notebook, how I brought you and my father together on paper. We laugh at the unlikelihood of your union, smug in our knowledge that it all came to pass. You help me keep my father alive. You encourage me to tell my own stories. You say that I must have inherited the words from my father. But when I close my eyes, searching for inspiration, it is your voice I hear chanting in the dark.

The Attic

The attic in Grandmother Power's home was a world of
dust, cobweb curtains, bashful spiders, and family history. In 1973 I was eleven years old and unable to get a
good night's sleep in that house. The few times I was
alone on the second floor, I had the feeling I was being
watched. *Don't be stupid,* I muttered to myself. But moments later I would run downstairs to join the others
just the same. Now I think it was the attic that unnerved
me. Perhaps I could feel it pressing down on the rest of
the house, burdened with the family archives and memories, a museum gone to ruin. My mother, however, was
intrigued by the idea of an attic. As a child she had lived
in a log cabin, single story, where room was scarce and
no one ever accumulated enough objects to need storage.

"We'll check out the attic tomorrow," Mom told me
on the night of our arrival.

The next day, as my father settled his ailing mother
in a nursing home just a few doors away from her own
address, I followed my mother up a narrow flight of
stairs. Our hands brushed oriental rugs that had been

rolled so tightly they resembled columns tipped on their sides—they lined the stair railing, wedged between the wooden rail and the wall. Mom and I stepped carefully across the floor so blanketed by dust it felt as though we were walking through powdery snow. We left tracks. We skirted the stout trunks and leaning stacks of books to stand together in a space free of clutter. We moved in a circle, a dance of confusion.

"Where should we begin," Mom said. It sounded more like a decision than a question. So we set to poking through the contents of as many trunks and boxes as we could reach. With eager hands we unearthed the only stories my mother didn't already know.

"Your father's people sure are pack rats," Mom said, sounding both critical and delighted. I smiled because she had said *Your father's people,* rather than *Your people*— a distinction of some importance to me.

All my life my mother had told me that I was late being born, I really took my time. I think I was just postponing the confusion. Half Yanktonnai Dakota (Sioux) and half white, I tortured myself with the obvious question: Whose side am I on anyway? We lived in Chicago, halfway between my two grandmothers, midway between two worlds. Grandmother Kelly lived on the Standing Rock Sioux Reservation in North Dakota, and Grandmother Power lived in Albany, New York. Grandmother Kelly was three years old when Sitting Bull was killed, and remembered seeing the wagon that brought his body to the agency for burial. Grandmother Power graduated from Smith College and was later invited to join the Daughters of the American Revolution, though she declined. These remarkable ladies were never brought together while they were alive, so they could meet only in me.

I felt distinctly Indian as my mother and I toiled in the attic, uncovering old secrets in letters, treasured mementos, faces in tintypes, names in bibles, unread books. It was all so unfamiliar to us it was completely fascinating.

Among the pages my mother rescued from oblivion was a legal document that recorded the events surrounding the murder of my ancestor, John M'Gilmore.

> *From the Plea Roll, in the reign of King Edward II, 1319: Robert Walsh was indicted at Waterford for killing John, son of Ivor M'Gilmore, and pledged that the said John was Irish, and that it was no felony to kill an Irishman.*
>
> *The King's attorney (John Fitz Robert le Poer) replied that M'Gilmore was an Ostman of Waterford, descended of Gerald M'Gilmore and that all his posterity and kinsmen were entitled to the law of Englishmen by the grant of Henry Fitz Empress, which he (the attorney) produced.*
>
> *And issue being joined, the jury found that on the first invasion of the English, Reginald the Dane, then ruler of Waterford, drew three great*

iron chains across the river to bar the passage of the King's fleet; but being conquered and taken by the English, he was for this tried and hanged by sentence of the King's court at Waterford with all his officers.

They further found that King Henry the Second [who reigned between 1154 and 1189] *banished all the then inhabitants of the town except Gerald M'Gilmore, who joined the English, and dwelt at that time in a tower over against the Church of the Friars.*

Mom chuckled to herself as she read the form. "People are crazy, aren't they? It was no felony to kill an Irishman, so they proved he was an Ostman. Well, we can certainly relate. There have been times when it wasn't a felony to kill an Indian either."

My mother was mesmerized; she had released a legion of ghosts, a chain of lives. Our faces were smudged and our hair was powdered with dust; we began to perspire as the afternoon heat gathered in the room, although we couldn't be sure it was solely the work of the sun. Together my mother and I had invoked the spirits of my white ancestors—they heard their names spoken aloud for the first time in centuries. And who could blame them for thronging to that cluttered garret, jostling for elbow room and a comfortable perch? Their lonely breath filled the gabled space, leaving us less air to breathe, less room to maneuver. I can smile now at the irony: the Indians were prowling through the attic on a voyage of discovery, exhuming my dead Pilgrim fathers. Several of my ancestors had helped form the original colony in Massachusetts, one of them had signed the Declaration of Independence, a number of them had fought as patriots in the American Revolution, and one crafty collector had diligently acquired the autographs of the main players in the Civil War.

My mother was overwhelmed by the stories and the artifacts; she called out to me again and again: "Come take a look! *This* is your heritage too."

But in the end we were seduced by the memory of a young woman who had not gone to battle, been elected to public office, or founded an institution of higher learning as had so many of the others. It was late in the day when we came across the plain wooden box that contained her life. Her name was Josephine Parkhurst Gilmore, and she was born on October 8, 1841. She had been taken in as a child by the Parkhursts, who later adopted her when she was eighteen. She lived with her adoptive parents in Newton Centre, Massachusetts; her father was a minister, and she would marry Joseph Henry Gilmore (my great-great-grandfather), pastor of the Baptist Church of Fisherville (now Penacook), New Hampshire. The wooden box contained a packet of letters Josephine had written to her parents, and a lock of her red-brown hair—the same dark shade as my own.

Later we would find her wedding dress crumpled inside a paper bag. I think it had been ivory silk trimmed with creamy white lace, but now it was the color of weak tea. We uncovered her tiny matching slippers—the satin covers and ribbon laces were still intact, and the soles unblemished. She must have worn them just the one time. The wedding shoes were so small and narrow my mother and I could barely manage to slip our hands inside them.

My mother studied the letters right there in the attic, beneath the faint light of a single bulb. She read me her favorite passages aloud, and I peered over her shoulder at the magnificent loops of Josephine's artful script.

"I wish I could write like that," I murmured.

Josephine's character seemed to us sunny and fine. She aspired to goodness and confided to her mother at age seventeen: *Sometimes I can hardly believe that I am indeed a child of God. For when I consider all His benefits and how unmindful I am of them—it seems only just that He should cut me off.*

Josephine was deeply grateful to her parents for taking her in as a small child and raising her as their own. She told them: *I think much of you and dear Father. You don't know how I feel toward you both when I think of all of your kindness for me, my heart is big with gratitude often times when I can't speak. I often shudder when I think of what*

I might have been if you had not had compassion for me. God will reward you for it. I never can.

Mom was tickled to learn that Josephine and her husband honeymooned in Niagara Falls, like so many couples after them. Josephine was nineteen years old and "Harry" twenty-seven when they married, and their wedding trip was "glorious":

> *In the short time I have been here I have got quite tanned up. I have not as yet ascended any of the mountains about here. I don't think I shall feel in any hurry about it—while there is so much to be seen at the foot of them.*
>
> *Harry, myself and a Mr. and Mrs. Thompson, a very pleasant couple from Boston, went together to the Flume, Pool and Basin. We had a charming excursion—such scenery and such climbing I never saw. We went clear through the Flume as far as we could go and came down outside of it. Then we took a charming walk through the woods, part of the way logs serving us for bridges and after going down a very steep pair of stairs we came to the Pool. I never enjoyed anything more. Everything was so wild, so grand and so wonderful. Everything said as plain as could be said: Behold the works of God.*
>
> *There was a great old man at the Pool who paddled us about in his boat. He is quite a philosopher in his way, and contends that the earth*

is hollow and has a map to explain to people his
theory. Some wicked wag who knew the old man's
eccentricities wrote a letter purporting to be from
Queen Victoria and sent it to him—the most ri-
diculous letter it is that ever was seen, but he takes
it for truth and has facsimile copies of it for sale.
I'll send you pretty soon. The original he keeps in
a glass case.

I laughed at the mention of the elderly gentleman and his grand theory, but my mother said, "I wish we had that letter." He was clearly the sort of person she would enjoy meeting. Mom gasped as she read the paragraph a few lines farther down: *General Peirce and Hawthorne, the author of "Marble Faun," have been here. Harry seemed to be quite a pet with them. They wanted him to go fishing with them, so he went early this morning.*

"That's Nathaniel Hawthorne she's talking about!" Mom told me. "And he considered your great-great-grandfather a pet."

It was hard for me to imagine the stern, bewhiskered Joseph Henry Gilmore I had seen in photographs as anything but a solemn cleric, though there were indications of poetry in his blood, for he penned the lyrics to my favorite hymn, "He Leadeth Me."

During the next year my great-great-grandparents traveled extensively, and in her letters Josephine described trips to Brooklyn and Philadelphia. She was greatly impressed with the Liberty Bell. In all her travels Josephine's parents were never far from her thoughts. From Philadelphia she wrote: *Evening finds me in Mr. Watson's office to write just a little to my dear ones at home. I have been showing your daguerrotypes to the Watsons today and I shouldn't want to tell you the compliments which were paid you. I would like so much to see the dear originals tonight. I hope you are well and happy. I think of you many times a day.*

Finally, in 1862, Josephine was home in New Hampshire for a time. My mother's voice softened as she read a letter from this period: *I wish you could look out of my window for a few minutes and see the clouds come sailing up the north. Yesterday I went on a delightful jaunt to see some cattails—on the way I picked and had picked for me over fifty Indian pipe flowers which are very rare. Then I picked a lot of myrtle, wild myrtle; it is like ours only more graceful, and with these I trimmed my hair and Aunt Nancy's. I have my hair trimmed with one thing and another, every night. I wish you might have seen the leaves I had the other night—maple they were—some of them were a deep green with red spots and stripes in them, others pure red, etc., beautifully turned by the frost. There are quantities of beautiful things here to dress my hair with—if one will look for them.*

The attic was growing dark and I was suddenly weary of my great-great-grandmother's reasonable voice. *Was she never persnickety?* I wondered. *Was she never cross?*

"Listen to this," Mom said, laughing. With great relief I heard the following censure: *Sallie Smith and I hardly speak to each other now. She snubbed me in the most pointed manner when I first came, until she found I was getting more attention paid me than she was, but then it was too late and I had had enough of her ways, and I just avoid her. I treat her politely, but no more. She is generally disliked and no wonder; her "stuckupishness" don't go down with anyone. She is a great hypocrite and a mischief maker.*

Josephine Parkhurst Gilmore wasn't perfect after all. This was an ancestor I could accept as family.

Shortly before leaving my grandmother's attic, Mom reached the last letters at the bottom of the box. They had been written in 1863. We quickly learned that Josephine was pregnant and her baby due at the end of September. In August she caught a cold she couldn't shake, and the girl begged her mother to come for a visit:

> *In addition to my cold I have the old complaint that summer brings. Of course I am weak, very. I try to keep up good courage and I haven't fairly broken down yet, but it is hard work. I have sent a telegram to father this morning and Lucy is still in Concord waiting for an answer to it. The Browns are all at home now. So you may feel safe about me I shall have good care.*
>
> *I wish you could be with me my last month. I*

think I need you as much then as at the time, and perhaps more. I don't seem to have any heart to take hold and get things ready. I may feel differently when I get better though. It would be so nice to have you here to arrange with me.

Two days later she mailed another entreaty:

I don't want to alarm you but I feel as if I must have you with me. I wanted to send for you but felt as if it would be perhaps foolish to do so, but Mrs. John Brown thinks I ought to. She has been with me all the afternoon rubbing and bathing me and wants me to send for the doctor but I had rather not, but I will send for you. Harry can't get back before the last of next week and with worrying about him and feeling really sick from this heavy cold, I don't feel safe to be alone. I can't sleep nights and really I am miserable and at this time I think I am not safe in being alone. Now won't you please come up and stay this week with me? I will pay your expenses very willingly. Won't you come up on the early train Tuesday?

At any rate I shall look forward to your being with me and that will help me to feel a little better. Father will be willing I know under the circumstances to let you come. I am not in the habit of complaining, you know, and I would not send for you now if I could get along without you. I have taken to my bed this afternoon—I have tried to sit

up until I have lost all backbone. I am so sorry this
cold should come just now. Now don't disappoint
your daughter.

"Why doesn't she go?!" I wailed, caught up in the
drama. "It wasn't that far, was it?"

"No," Mom answered. "Just Boston to New
Hampshire, though it took a lot longer to get around
in those days." Perhaps she noticed my distress, for she
patted my hand. "I would be there in a second."

Mary Parkhurst did make the journey, it turned out,
though she only stayed for a few days. In her final letter,
Josephine again urged her mother to visit.

September 6, 1863

My dear mother,

I wish you could be with me today. I am not
feeling well at all and as Aunt Maria has not yet
returned, I am a bit lonely while Harry is at
church. I have managed to take a little more cold
and I am so stiff and sore that I can hardly get up
or down. I am getting very clumsy anyway—It
seems as if I could hardly wait three weeks longer.
I want you to be on hand early, Mother.

My room isn't put in order yet for the reason
the stove man has been away and so I couldn't
have the stove set. I thought it best to make only
one job of it.

Harry was in Boston last week. He was obliged to go to his cousin Fred's funeral. He went down in the early train Friday and back in the early train Saturday. He had no time to go to see father. What do you think he brought me home? A basket of delicious fruit, pears, plums and grapes. They were luscious.

It seemed like old times at Newton. When I used to be ill, don't you know how very thoughtful he always was. If our lives are only spared what a happy family ours will be after the little one comes. I do pray that God may grant to us a dear little child and good health.

Mrs. John Brown has been in today to see me. She seems to take a great interest in me. I think a good deal of her judgement—she has had experience you know.

I will write you again next week, but am too tired to prolong this epistle. Come up as soon as you can. With a great deal of love to father and yourself.

I am, your daughter,
Josie Gilmore

There are two or three plants I want you to buy for me to bring up with you; a mahunia, a white camilia what they call candidissima and a plant called colisium ivy. Father can buy these in Boston you know, and you can bring them up with you, can't you? They will of course all be small plants.

*Goodbye again. Love to the Smiths when you see
them.*

On September 9, Josephine gave birth to Joseph
Henry Gilmore Jr., and on September 11, she died.

My mother and I huddled together in the attic, two
more shadows lost in the disorder. Mom returned the
letters and the lock of hair to the heavy box. We folded
the brittle wedding dress as gently as we could, smoothing a century of wrinkles.

"Her little boy must have kept these things so he
could feel close to the mother he never knew," Mom
said. "He was your Daddy's grandfather, and Daddy
worshipped him. He was gentle and mischievous, and
loved your father."

When Mom and I left the hushed attic it was as if
we had returned to life, the way I have felt on emerging
from church into afternoon light. We rescued the
family papers and the stories they contained, and we
still tell them to one another, though my mother tells
them best. We know what happened to "Harry" and his
son, and for us it is like looking into the future. Two
years after Josephine died, Joseph Henry Gilmore married Miss Lucy Brown, who had been a dear friend of
Josephine's and one of her nurses at the end. She was
a good mother to Josephine's child and gave him five
siblings.

My grandmother died three months after Mom and

I explored her attic, and the house was sold. It has been twenty-two years since that last visit.

My mother is proud of her Dakota forebears and the Sioux Nation she comes from, but she has encouraged me to find both sides of myself, and so, undiminished, I have become whole.

"You gave me a great gift," I should tell my mother the next time I telephone. But it is hard for me to say these things.

— ⁓

My mother and I visited Josephine Parkhurst Gilmore's grave at the start of my sophomore year in college. I remember I was bored and a little irritated as we wandered through the old section of Newton Cemetery. I was anxious to meet a new roommate and wanted the school year to begin, I couldn't be bothered with ancestral spirits who were lonesome for company.

"She is here somewhere," my mother told me. "Concentrate."

I don't know why we didn't go through proper channels, why we didn't visit an office and ask for a map of the burial plots—there must have been records. But we conducted this search on our own, without benefit of bureaucracy, and I felt a little like a skeptic handling a dousing stick. I squinted at the worn gravestones, following a path my mother suggested, and just minutes after we stepped from the car, I found Josephine settled between her parents.

"Over here," I called to my mother a little gruffly. It had all worked out just as she'd promised. I had found my relative so easily because she longed to be discovered and remembered. But I couldn't stand for my mother to be right.

"It's just a coincidence," I mumbled.

"Just think, you've found her," Mom whispered. "Josephine Parkhurst Gilmore, this is your great-great-granddaughter." My mother made the introductions and I probably squirmed a little, peeked over my shoulder to be certain we were alone, unobserved. I was poor company.

Mom cried a little. "It's the Irish in me," she teased, and she brushed a hand across the face of Josephine's marker. "Let's find a stone to remind us of this place." We uncovered a flat triangular rock, and Mom wrapped it in Kleenex tissue.

I know my mother must have told Josephine that I was a sophomore at Harvard because it wouldn't be rude to brag to another relative. Surely she mentioned we were Indian, Dakotas, and wondered what Josephine would make of that. She could have lectured the girl, telling her that on September 3, 1863—just three days before Josephine Parkhurst Gilmore penned her last letter—the peaceful village of my great-great-grandfather,

Chief Two Bear, had been attacked by Generals Sibley and Sully, and our Yanktonnai band nearly wiped out.

My mother has described the scene so vividly I sometimes think she must have been there, urging the dogs to run swiftly from the slaughter, dragging babies strapped to miniature travois behind them. Her nostrils quiver when she tells me that the soldiers burned the camp and the winter stores of food, and I know she can smell the fragrance of that wasted buffalo meat and taste the melting tallow.

But all my mother said was: "I hope your mother was there at the end. I know you weren't alone, but your husband or a friend wouldn't be the same comfort, would they? There are times when only a mother will do."

Yes, I can tell her now, *there are times.* I can agree because I am older. After all my education I have finally learned that I will never know as much as my mother. I stand happily in her shadow, no longer annoyed by her faith and imagination. I ask her to repeat the stories. I strain to hear her voice.

And the next time my mother visits me in Cambridge, Massachusetts, I will suggest we return to Newton Cemetery. We will wander through the old section, patiently searching for the young lady we visited once before. This time I will be more polite, ready with presents I offer my great-great-grandmother, who is now twelve years my junior.

"Mom, look," I will whisper as I unwrap the papers.
The wild myrtle is a brilliant blue, it should look fine
twisted in the intricate crown of Josephine's brown
hair; the white camellias are soft, snowy, and will cover
her slight figure like a blanket of lace.

Chicago Waters

My mother used to say that by the time I was an old woman, Lake Michigan would be the size of a silver dollar. She pinched her index finger with her thumb to show me the pitiful dimensions.

"People will gather around the tiny lake, what's left of it, and cluck over a spoonful of water," she told me.

I learned to squint at the 1967 shoreline until I had carved away the structures and roads built on landfill, and could imagine the lake and its city as my mother found them in 1942 when she arrived in Chicago. I say *the lake and its city* rather than *the city and its lake,* because my mother taught me another secret: the city of Chicago belongs to Lake Michigan.

But which of my mother's pronouncements to believe? That Chicago would swallow the midwestern sea, smother it in concrete, or that the lake wielded enough strength to outpolitick even Mayor Richard J. Daley?

Mayor Daley Sr. is gone now, but the lake remains, alternately tranquil and riled, changing colors like a mood ring. I guess we know who won.

When my mother watches the water from her lake-side apartment building, she still sucks in her breath. "You have to respect the power of that lake," she tells me. And I do now. I do.

I was fifteen years old when I learned that the lake did not love me or hate me, but could claim me, nevertheless. I was showing off for a boy, my best friend, Tommy, who lived in the same building. He usually accompanied me when I went for a swim, but on this particular day he decided the water was too choppy. I always preferred the lake when it was agitated because its temperature warmed, transforming it into a kind of jacuzzi.

Tommy is right, I thought, once I saw the looming swells that had looked so unimpressive from the twelfth floor. Waves crashed against the breakwater wall and the metal ladder that led into and out of the lake like the entrance to the deep end of a swimming pool.

I shouldn't do this, I told myself, but I noticed Tommy watching me from his first-floor window. "I'm not afraid," I said to him under my breath. "I bet you think that I'll chicken out just because I'm a girl."

It had been a hot summer of dares, some foolish, some benign. Sense was clearly wanting. I took a deep breath and leapt off the wall into the turmoil, since the ladder was under attack. How did I think I would get out of the water? I hadn't thought that far. I bobbed to the surface and was instantly slapped in the face. I was beaten by water, smashed under again and again, until I began choking because I couldn't catch my breath.

I'm going to die now, I realized, and my heart filled with sorrow for my mother, who had already lost a husband and would now lose a daughter. I fought the waves, struggled to reach the air and the light, the sound of breakers swelling in my ears, unnaturally loud, like the noise of judgment day. *Here we go,* I thought.

Then I surprised myself, becoming unusually calm. I managed a quick gasp of breath and plunged to the bottom of the lake, where the water was a little quieter. I swam to the beach next door, remaining on the lake floor until I reached shallow waters. I burst to the surface then, my lungs burning, and it took me nearly five minutes to walk fifteen feet, knocked off balance as I was by waves that sucked at my legs. This beach now belongs to my mother and the other shareholders in her building, property recently purchased and attached to their existing lot. But in 1977 it was owned by someone else, and a barbed-wire fence separated the properties. I ended my misadventure by managing to climb over the sharp wire.

I remained downstairs until I stopped shaking. Tommy no longer watched me from his window, bored by my private games, unaware of the danger. I didn't tell my mother what had happened until hours later. I was angry at myself for being so foolish, so careless with my life, but I was never for a moment angry at the lake. I didn't come to fear it either, though it is a mighty force that drops 923 feet in its deepest heart. I understand that it struck indifferently; I was neither target nor friend. My life was my own affair, to lose or to save. Once I stopped struggling with the great lake, I flowed through it, and was expelled from its hectic mouth.

My mother still calls Fort Yates, North Dakota, *home,* despite the fact that she has lived in Chicago for nearly fifty-five years. She has taken me to visit the Standing Rock Sioux Reservation, where she was raised, and although a good portion of it was flooded during the construction of the Oahe Dam, she can point to hills and buttes and creeks of significance. The landscape there endures, outlives its inhabitants. But I am a child of the city, where landmarks are man-made, impermanent. My attachments to place are attachments to people, my love for a particular area only as strong as my local relationships. I have lived in several cities and will live in several more. I visit the country with curiosity and trepidation, a clear foreigner, out of my league, and envy the connection my mother has to a dusty town, the peace she finds on a prairie. It is a kind of religion, her devotion to Proposal Hill and the Missouri River, a sacred bond that I can only half-understand. If

I try to see the world through my mother's eyes, find the point where my own flesh falls to earth, I realize my home is Lake Michigan, the source of so many lessons.

As a teenager I loved to swim in the dark, to dive beneath the surface where the water was as black as the sky. The lake seemed limitless and so was I, an arm, a leg, a wrist, a face indistinguishable from the wooden boards of a sunken dock, from the sand I squeezed between my toes. I always left reluctantly, loath to become a body again and to feel more acutely the oppressive pull of gravity.

My father was the one who taught me to swim, with his usual patience and clear instructions. First he helped me float, his hands beneath my back and legs, his torso shading me from the sun. Next he taught me to flutter-kick, and I tried to make as much noise as possible. I dog-paddled in circles as a little girl, but my father swam in a straight line perpendicular to shore, as if he were trying to leave this land forever. Just as he had left New York state after a lifetime spent within its borders—easily, without regret. His swim was always the longest, the farthest. Mom and I would watch him as we lounged on our beach towels, nervous that a boat might clip him. It was a great relief to see him turn around and coast in our direction.

"Here he comes," Mom would breathe. "He's coming back now."

My father also showed me how to skip a stone across the water. He was skillful and could make a flat rock bounce like a tiny, leaping frog, sometimes five or six hops before it sank to the bottom. It was the only time I could imagine this distinguished, silver-haired gentleman as a boy, and I laughed at him affectionately because the difference in our years collapsed.

My mother collects stones in her backyard—a rough, rocky beach in South Shore. She looks for pebbles drilled with holes—not pits or mere scratches, but tiny punctures worn clear through the stone.

"I can't leave until I find at least one," she tells me.

"Why?" I ask. I've asked her more than once because I am forgetful.

"There are powerful spirits in these stones, trying to tunnel their way out."

Ah, that explains the holes. What I do not ask is why she selects them, these obviously unquiet souls, why she places them in a candy dish or a basket worn soft as flannel. What good can it do them? What good can it do her to unleash such restless forces on the quiet of her rooms?

I finger my mother's collection when I'm home for a visit. I have even pressed a smooth specimen against my cheek. The touch is cool. I believe it could draw a fever, the object mute and passive in my hand. At first I think there is a failing on my part since I cannot hear what my mother hears, and then I decide that the spirits caught in these stones have already escaped. I imagine them returning to the lake, to the waves that pushed them onto the beach and washed their pebble flesh, because it is such a comfort to return to water.

And then I remember my own weightless immersion, how my body becomes a fluid spirit when I pull myself underwater, where breath stops. And I remember gliding along the lake's sandy bottom as a child, awed by the orderly pattern of its dunes. Lake Michigan is cold, reliably cold, but occasionally I passed through warm pockets, abrupt cells of tepid water that always came as a surprise. I am reminded of cold spots reputedly found in haunted houses, and I wonder if these warm areas are evidence of my lost souls?

A young man drowned in these waters behind my mother's building some years ago. Mom was seated in a lawn chair, visiting with another tenant on the terrace. They sat together, facing the lake so they could watch its activity, though it was calm that day, uninteresting. A young man stroked into view, swimming parallel to the shore and headed north. He was close enough for them to read his features; he was fifteen feet away from shallow depths, where he could have stood with his head above water. He called to them a reasonable question in a calm voice. He wanted to know how far south he was. Seventy-three hundred, they told him. He moved on. A marathon swimmer, the women decided. But eventually my mother and her friend noticed his absence, scanned the horizon, unable to see his bobbing head and strong arms. They alerted the doorman, who called the police. The young man was found near the spot where he'd made his cordial inquiry.

"Why didn't he cry for help? Why didn't he signal his distress?" my mother asked the response unit.

"This happens all the time with men," she was told. "They aren't taught to cry for help."

So he is there too, the swimmer, a warm presence in cold water or a spirit in a stone.

⌒ ⌒

I have gone swimming in other places—a chlorinated pool in Hollywood, the warm waters of the Caribbean, the Heart River in North Dakota—only to be disappointed and emerge unrefreshed. I am too used to Lake Michigan and its eccentricities. I must have cold, fresh water. I must have the stinking corpses of silver alewives floating on the surface as an occasional nasty surprise, discovered dead and never alive. I must have sailboats on the horizon and steel mills on the southern shore, golf balls I can find clustered around submerged pilings (shot from the local course), and breakwater boulders heavy as tombs lining the beach. I must have sullen life-guards who whistle anyone bold enough to stand in three feet of water, and periodic arguments between wind and water, which produce tearing waves and lake-spattered windows.

When I was little, maybe seven or eight, my parents and I went swimming in a storm. The weather was mild when we first set out, but the squall arrived quickly, without warning, as often happens in the Midwest. I remember we swam anyway, keeping an eye on the lightning not yet arrived from the north. There was no one to stop us, since we were dipping into deep water between beaches, in an area that was unpatrolled. The water was warmer than usual, the same temperature as the air, and when the rain wet the sky I leapt up and down in the growing waves, unable to feel the difference between air and water, lake and rain. The three of us played together that time, even my father remained near shore rather than striking east to swim past the white buoys. We were joined in this favorite element, splashing, ducking. I waved my arms over my head. My father pretended to be a great whale, heavy in the surf, now and then spouting streams of water from his mouth. He chased me. My mother laughed.

Dad died in 1973, when I was eleven years old, before my mother and I moved to the apartment on the lake. We always thought it such a shame he didn't get to make that move with us. He would so have enjoyed finding Lake Michigan in his backyard.

We buried him in Albany, New York, because that is where he was raised. My mother was born in North Dakota, and I was born between them, in Chicago. There is a good chance we shall not all rest together, our stories playing out in different lands. But I imagine that if a rendezvous is possible, and my mother insists it is, we will find one another in this great lake, this small sea that rocks like a cradle.

SUSAN POWER is an enrolled member of the Standing Rock Sioux tribe and a native Chicagoan. She is a graduate of Harvard College, Harvard Law School, and the Iowa Writer's Workshop, and the recipient of a James Michener Fellowship, Radcliffe Bunting Institute Fellowship, and Princeton Hodder Fellowship. Her first novel, *The Grass Dancer*, was published in 1994 and awarded the PEN/ Hemingway Prize. Her short fiction has appeared in the *Atlantic Monthly*, *Paris Review*, *Voice Literary Supplement*, *Ploughshares*, *Story*, and *The Best American Short Stories 1993*. She lives in St. Paul, Minnesota.

WINNERS OF THE MILKWEED NATIONAL FICTION PRIZE

To order books or for more information, contact Milkweed at (800) 520-6455 or visit our website (www.milkweed.org).

ROOFWALKER
Susan Power
(2002)

HELL'S BOTTOM, COLORADO
Laura Pritchett
(2001)

FALLING DARK
Tim Tharp
(1999)

TIVOLEM
Victor Rangel-Ribeiro
(1998)

THE TREE OF RED STARS
Tessa Bridal
(1997)

THE EMPRESS OF ONE
Faith Sullivan
(1996)

CONFIDENCE OF THE HEART
David Schweidel
(1995)

MONTANA 1948
Larry Watson
(1993)

LARABI'S OX
Tony Ardizzone
(1992)

AQUABOOGIE
Susan Straight
(1990)

BLUE TAXIS
Eileen Drew
(1989)

GANADO RED
Susan Lowell
(1988)

MORE FICTION FROM
MILKWEED EDITIONS

JOIN US

Since its genesis as *Milkweed Chronicle* in 1979, Milkweed has helped hundreds of emerging writers reach their readers. Thanks to the generosity of foundations and of individuals like you, Milkweed Editions is able to continue its nonprofit mission of publishing books chosen on the basis of literary merit—on how they impact the human heart and spirit—rather than on how they impact the bottom line. That's a miracle that our readers have made possible.

In addition to purchasing Milkweed books, you can join the growing community of Milkweed supporters. Individual contributions of any amount are both meaningful and welcome. Contact us for a Milkweed catalog or log on to www.milkweed.org and click on "About Milkweed," then "Why Join Milkweed," to find out about our donor program, or simply call (800) 520-6455 and ask about becoming one of Milkweed's contributors. As a nonprofit press, Milkweed belongs to you, the community. Milkweed's board, its staff, and especially the authors whose careers you help launch thank you for reading our books and supporting our mission in any way you can.

Interior design by Dale Cooney
Typeset in Legacy Serif 11/15
by Stanton Publication Services
Printed on acid-free 55# Natural Odyssey Hibulk paper
by Friesen Coporation